# llama llama misses mama

## Anna Dewdney

VIKING

Llama Llama, warm in bed.
Wakey, wakey, sleepyhead!

Llama school begins **today!**
Time to learn and time to play!

Make the bed and
find some clothes.

Brush the teeth
and blow the nose.

Eat some breakfast.
Clean the plate.

**Whoops!**
Oh my—
we're running late!

Drive to school
and park the car.

Tell the teacher
who you are.

Meet new faces.
Hear new names.
See new places.
Watch new games.

YOU CAME BACK!!!

Teacher gets a good-bye hug.

Wave to friends on reading rug.

Climb the playhouse with the slide.
See if Mama fits inside.

Lots to show and lots to say!
Back again another day. . . .

Llama finds out something new—

He loves Mama . . .

# 6

**Six**

# Doggie tricks!

# Seven . . .

**7**

**8**

Eight

# Social Habits, Design and Structure

Furniture reveals many confidential things about the social life of the past and present; like architecture it amplifies and illuminates the story of civilization in nearly every country, and provides an intimate, personal record of habits, postures, manners, fashions and follies. For example, the large, adjustable chairs, designed with what is most appropriately called 'dimensional abundance', disclose how restless and fidgety many people are today, and how modern Europeans and Americans are pampered by upholstered furniture to an extent that would have seemed incredible two hundred years ago. Contemporary easy chairs are expected to accommodate constant changes of position by their users, unlike the high-backed winged easy chairs of the late seventeenth and eighteenth centuries that were made for people who sat upright to preserve their dignity and remained still to avoid disturbing the set of their wigs or the powder in their hair. Some of the comforts and discomforts of life in the Middle Ages are illustrated by a cupboard with doors pierced for ventilation, known as an aumbry or ambry, and, after the sixteenth century, as a livery cupboard, for people then defeated 'night starvation' by taking rations of food and drink to their bedrooms. These consisted of bread, beer and spiced wine, and were called 'liveries'. The habit of taking an early morning snack from what remained of the liveries was condemned by Thomas Tusser, who wrote:

> 'Some slovens from sleeping, no sooner be up
> but hand is in aumbrie, and nose in the cup.'

That couplet appeared in his book, *Five Hundred Points of good husbandry united to as many good huswifere*, published in 1573; but his view seems rather harsh, for in that

1

*Left :* **Small aumbry for 'liveries'. The bed stands in the angle made by two walls, with the canopy (or tester) suspended from the ceiling. Reproduced in Henry Shaw's** *Specimens of Ancient Furniture* **from a fifteenth century manuscript.**
*Right :* **An almery, or wall aumbry, in Lincoln Cathedral,** *circa* **1200.** *After Parker.*

tea-less age something heartening in the way of a drink was necessary to combat the bitter chill of bedrooms in winter, for they were usually far away from the fire in the great hall, often the only source of heat in a house.

From the design of beds we learn about the thousand-year-long battle for warmth and privacy in England and northern Europe. For many centuries beds were structurally dependent on walls and built like cabins along the sides of the great hall in Anglo-Saxon and Scandinavian houses, closed at night by wooden doors or curtains of leather or fabric. This partnership with the wall persisted throughout the Middle Ages, and later the bed was incorporated as an architectural feature, like the early seventeenth century Dutch example shown opposite page 1. The icy temperature of bedrooms was overcome by enclosing the bed with thick curtains, which transformed it into a warm, stifling room within a room. Even in the early nineteenth century unheated bedrooms were usual; when Sam Weller brought warm water into Mr Pickwick's bedroom at Dingley Dell on Christmas morning he told his master that the water in the wash-hand basin was 'a mask o' ice'; and heavily curtained beds were in use until the end of that century. A stuffy atmosphere seemed safer than night air, which was feared alike by Plantagenet kings and Victorian householders.

Seats and cupboards also depended on walls, and recesses were sunk in the thickness of stonework and fitted with hinged doors like an almery in a mediaeval church. (An almery, or wall aumbry, in a church was placed near the altar and used for sacramental vessels.) Forms and benches usually stood against a wall, on which a strip of fabric called a dorcer was hung to provide a back rest, and seats with lockers under them occupied bay windows. The interior of a fifteenth century hall, reproduced in colour

Carved seat or head-rest, supported by a human figure. From the Congo (Bambala tribe). *Reproduced by courtesy of the Trustees of the British Museum.*

opposite page 123, shows a chair of state and seats ranged against a wall, with the stepped shelves of an open plate cupboard, the mediaeval equivalent of a cocktail bar, as a built-in feature. When furniture became independent of the wall, and could be described as free-standing, mobility in furnishing was possible, which helped to change social habits. In the dining parlours of the late sixteenth century, for instance, host and hostess and their guests no longer sat at one side of the table with their backs to the wall as they did in the Middle Ages; the table was moved to the middle of the room, and host and hostess sat at either end, with their guests along the sides. This reflected a change in manners, which had become less formal, and a greater appreciation of the art of conversation, that grew less stilted and altogether easier after such a revolution in seating arrangements.

These are a few examples of social habits and amenities recorded by furniture; but differences in national and racial habits are also disclosed by the dimensions and design of such articles as seats and tables. The races of mankind sit in different ways, not because there are any anatomical differences between Asiatics, whites or Negroes, but because they have developed special cultural habits. Differences in posture may be established by the social order, as in Ancient Egypt, where the ruling classes sat upright on chairs or stools like Europeans, but the Fellahin, the peasants and slaves, squatted on the floor. The Chinese, Japanese, Burmese, Hindus and some nations of the Middle East sit with their legs comfortably arranged in a horizontal position, a posture that affects the design of their furniture, for they live at a lower eye-level than Europeans, consequently their tables have shorter legs than European tables, and their stools, raised only a few inches above the floor, have feet instead of legs. In the Middle and Far East mats or cushions are often used in place of stools or chairs.

The progress of skill in furniture-making, the appetite for luxury, and the discovery of comfort are all revealed by the evolution of such familiar, everyday things as chairs and tables, beds and chests. During a period of perhaps eight thousand years, furniture has developed from crude and clumsy attempts to make life a little easier and more secure, by the invention of seats and receptacles, to the ornamental achievements of the French rococo style two centuries ago and the luxurious upholstery of the present day.

Nearly all articles of free-standing furniture are variations of two basic shapes: a

3

Writing table of deal veneered with ebony and Boulle marquetry of tortoiseshell and brass. The bronze mounts are chased and gilt, and the top inlaid with black morocco leather. A typical example of the ornate furniture made for the French aristocracy before the Revolution. *Reproduced by courtesy of the Trustees of the Wallace Collection. Crown copyright.*

platform or a box. Stools, benches, chairs, couches, beds and tables are platforms elevated on feet or legs or underframing, on which you sit, lie, or put things; chests, cupboards and wardrobes are boxes for storing anything from linen and clothes to food, wine, drinking vessels, documents or money; while there are combinations of platforms and boxes, such as sideboards, buffets, dressing tables, writing desks, also chairs, settles and stools with hinged seats and receptacles below. The most elementary form of seat was a solid block of wood or stone; the earliest structural invention in furniture followed the bright idea of placing a flat stone on two others of equal height, and then applying the principle to wood, with a roughly-hewn board supported by three or four uprights driven into the ground.

Whether furniture is made to meet the simple needs of people in a tribal stage of civilization, like the Zulus under Chaka in the early nineteenth century, or to satisfy the complex and luxurious tastes of a sophisticated, aristocratic society of the kind that flourished in France and England during the eighteenth century, those basic forms, platform and box, are unchanged. The most highly valued possession of a primitive tribe may be a carved seat, used exclusively by the chief and therefore a symbol of authority, like the specimen from the Congo on page 3 which doubles the part of seat and head-rest; the most conspicuous treasures of a national or private collection may be as ornate as the writing table veneered with ebony and Boulle marquetry above

4

5

Mahogany sideboard with ebony lines, designed by Gordon Russell in the late 1920s.

or the richly carved Master's chair of the Fruiterers' Company on page 5, but all three are platforms for supporting weight, while the modern mahogany sideboard designed by Gordon Russell above, the sixteenth century Italian marriage chest, and the late eighteenth century English hanging corner cupboard opposite, are obviously boxes. The gilt chiffonier on page 8, like other hanging shelves, consists of suspended platforms. The exceptions that cannot be classified as platforms or boxes are articles with specialized functions, such as mirrors, screens, wall sconces, girandoles, chandeliers, lamp standards and baby cages, like the example on page 9.

Wood, stone, metal and ivory have been used for furniture from the earliest times, with leather and fabrics as accessories; but wood, easily the most tractable and varied material, has remained so long in favour that until recently it was employed exclusively for the industrially-produced furniture of the present century. Wood has stimulated the skill and imagination of craftsmen since joinery, turnery and cabinet-making were invented at some remote period of Ancient Egyptian history. A tomb painting from Thebes, *circa* 1380 B.C., depicts joiners busy in a well-equipped workshop, comparable with the carpenters' shop shown in the mediaeval carving at the top of page 10. Egyptian woodworkers used, and most probably invented, the mortice and tenon joint, which

*Left:* A hanging corner cupboard in oak, with pilasters, frieze and drawer fronts veneered with mahogany, inlaid with thin lines of boxwood and ebony. English: made in the countryside. Second half of the eighteenth century. *In the possession of Mrs V. Atkins.*

*Below:* Marriage chest (Cassone), of cedar wood, carved and gilt with painted details. Italian (Venetian), *circa* 1520. *Reproduced by courtesy of the Victoria and Albert Museum. Crown copyright.*

A gilt chiffonier designed by the architect Henry Holland for the Duke of Bedford's temporary residence at Oakley, 1794. *In the collection of the late Sir Albert Richardson, PP. R.A., at Avenue House, Ampthill.*

gave stability to the frames of seats and receptacles such as chests. That joint consists of a cavity, the mortice, cut into a piece of wood, to receive the tenon, a projection cut on another piece of wood to fit exactly into the hollow space. Constructed furniture represented an enormous advance over solid seats, chipped into shape from a block of stone or hewn from a log of wood, or the primitive receptacles made from tree trunks hollowed by fire or chopped out with axes. Hollowing out a tree trunk is no more a structural technique than digging a hole in a hillside for shelter or enlarging a cave is architecture. Furniture design could not advance beyond an elementary stage until such crude methods were replaced by structural techniques, such as joinery, and supplemented by new, skilled ways of shaping wood, like the art of turnery. Progress in constructional knowledge was accompanied by a corresponding improvement in the efficiency and variety of tools; much of the knowledge which had accumulated in Ancient Egypt was passed on to other and later civilizations, and although it was not altogether lost, some of it had to be rediscovered by mediaeval craftsmen. Wood was scarce in Egypt, and although joiners and cabinet-makers used sycamore and acacia, which grew in the country, nearly all their work was done with cedar, imported from Syria. Wood was abundant in mediaeval Europe and England, so craftsmen had powers of selection and opportunities for studying the growth and character of timber that were denied to the ancient Egyptians, and this gave them—especially English craftsmen—a sympathetic understanding and love of wood that was to have a profound effect on design. The Egyptians attained a standard of competence in the construction of recep-

8

tacles, with horizontal members slotted into vertical posts and secured by pegs, so they could make furniture like the toilet chest on page 11, but they never progressed beyond that particular stage of structural stability or became adventurous as designers, like French, Flemish and English craftsmen in the Middle Ages. The Egyptian toilet chest of 1300 B.C. is structurally superior to the thirteenth century English oak boarded chest shown on the same page, for the latter consists of split or sawn planks, put together very simply and held in place by iron nails at the angles, helped out with oak pins, and braced at each end with cross-pieces. This chest, though crudely made, was structurally self-sufficient, unlike the hollowed-out chests that had to be strengthened with bands of iron. The next stage of development was panelled framing, which superseded plank construction and consisted of thin rectangular panels framed by vertical and horizontal members, known as stiles and rails. The joints were connected by mortice and tenon, and these joined chests of composite construction were strong, durable, far lighter than

**A baby cage of turned ash and mahogany. First half of the eighteenth century.** *Reproduced by courtesy of the Victoria and Albert Museum. Crown copyright.*

Misericord of carved oak, depicting the interior of a mediaeval carpenters' shop. One of thirteen from St Nicholas Chapel, King's Lynn, Norfolk. *Reproduced by courtesy of the Victoria and Albert Museum. Crown copyright.*

the earlier types and much better looking. They were introduced during the second half of the fifteenth century. The early seventeenth century example on page 13 shows how the central members of the framework, which were called muntins, have been lightened by smoothing off the angles with chamfers, and the bottom rail is also chamfered where it meets the panels.

Once woodworkers had solved the initial structural problems, the way was open for the imaginative application of the joined technique to other forms of furniture, to cupboards, tables, stools and chairs. The two English oak stools on page 14 illustrate the different applications of joined construction. The seat of the board-ended type at the top of the page is supported by two vertical boards, held in place by apron pieces, with ornamental piercing. Such stools were made in the late fifteenth and early sixteenth centuries, and this example, from the Victoria and Albert Museum, is incomplete, as the apron piece at the back is missing. The joined or joint stool on the lower part of the page has turned legs framed into a frieze rail which supports the seat, while stretchers link the legs below and give additional stability. The ends of the frieze rails are united to the top of each leg with a mortice and tenon joint, and the close-up view shows the heads of the dowels, the wooden pegs or pins, that secure the joint. Such stools were made in great numbers, usually in sets of six, from the mid-sixteenth to the end of the seventeenth century, and used for seating at dining tables; they also had an additional use as tables for small children who sat on low stools. The name buffet stool, which occurs in many contemporary inventories, was probably an alternative term. A later and

10

*Left :* Egyptian toilet chest, *circa* 1300 B.C. This belonged to Tutu, wife of the scribe Ani, and is from his tomb at Thebes. It contains a terra cotta pot and two alabaster vases holding ointments of different kinds; a piece of pumice stone; a double kohl-tube containing different eye paints for hot and cold weather; an ivory comb; a bronze dish for mixing cosmetics; three fibre jar tops, and a pair of gazelle-skin sandals. *Reproduced by courtesy of the Trustees of the British Museum.*

*Right :* Thirteenth century English oak boarded chest, constructed of split or sawn planks, and raised slightly above floor level. The ledge with the hinged lid on the far side is to accommodate sweet scented herbs. *Formerly in the collection of the late Robert Atkinson, F.R.I.B.A.*

11

totally different type of joined seat is the Italian chair of carved walnut shown on page 15. This is one of a pair, made in the first half of the seventeenth century. Loose cushions were generally used on the hard, flat seats of such stools and chairs. The joined armchair in oak on page 16, identical in structure with the joint stool on page 14, has front legs that are projected above seat level to form supports for the arms, which are socketed into them. Both stool and armchair combine joined construction with turned work. In the Middle Ages, turners were the principal chair-makers, not joiners, and they produced characteristic forms, like the thirteenth century triangular-seated example on page 17, taken from an illuminated manuscript in the Bodleian Library. Those forms persisted, and the Brewster type of mid-seventeenth century turned chair from New England reproduced on the same page, though separated by four hundred and fifty years from the earlier example, is an obvious descendant. (See also page 92.)

Mediaeval craftsmen were far more enterprising and imaginative than their predecessors in the ancient world. Although Egyptian furniture design, like Egyptian architecture, remained unchanged for thousands of years after the chief structural inventions had been made, the woodworkers of later times owed much to those pioneers who originated, before 2000 B.C., many of the techniques and perfected most of the tools that have been used ever since.

When wood was first shaped by cutting tools on a rotating surface, the long and lively history of turnery began. Almost certainly the lathe was invented and first used in Egypt, where turned work had, by the thirteenth century B.C., achieved an elegance and delicacy unsurpassed for another three thousand years. The toilet chest on page 11 has turned underframing, and the angle posts, continuing downwards as legs, have turned feet. The lathe was known and used in Assyria, Greece, the Roman and Byzantine Empires, and mediaeval Europe. The use of turned components in furniture increased the variety and lightness of many articles, especially seats and tables. Turnery has been used continuously for many centuries in Europe, Asia, Africa, and, since the seventeenth century, in North America. In common with such simple crafts as wickerwork, it has survived the decline and fall of civilizations. Materials have varied and changed, as the next chapter relates, but the basic woodworking crafts usually persist, even when opportunities for practising them are limited by war, conquest, revolution or economic collapse. Technical knowledge is harder to kill than any other kind, and is seldom subjected to religious, political or military persecution. Even Genghis Khan and Tamerlane spared skilled craftsmen when they devastated countries and sacked cities. But for opportunities to use their skill, craftsmen were dependent on customers who could pay for it, and when civilization decayed in large areas of fifth century Europe after the fall of the Western Roman Empire there was a shortage of money and customers. In such a twilit period of 'make-do and mend', knowledge passed down from father to son or master to apprentice is dimmed by disuse; all arts and crafts are limited because the world has shrunk, and petty, semi-barbaric states have replaced the prosperous free-trading area of a great Empire. A tool like a lathe could easily be forgotten in the course of a century, and in the dark ages between the end of Roman power and the rise of mediaeval civilization, the tools and skills of earlier ages were in active, day-to-day

Early seventeenth century English chest in oak, showing panelled construction. The central muntins and the top of the lower rail are chamfered. (See diagram below.) *In the possession of the author.*

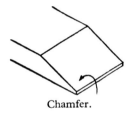

Chamfer.

use only in the Byzantine Empire and the Middle East. In the ninth and tenth centuries woodworkers in Western Europe had to make a fresh start, and over two hundred years elapsed before furniture-making became a recognized craft with specialized sub-divisions.

The carpenter was the craftsman originally responsible for all large-scale uses of timber, such as house-building, ship-building, erecting stockades round forts, and making the framework of siege-engines for attacking strongholds; much of his work was devoted to fortification and military needs. He became an expert on timber, converting into beams and planks the trees that foresters had felled and roughly trimmed. Building was his chief business, and when furniture was needed he knocked up rough benches and boarded chests, and fixed settles and bed-places against walls, thus establishing the partnership between furniture and architecture mentioned earlier. (In the Greek and Roman civilizations architecture and furniture design were related, but, as we shall see in chapter three, that was an ornamental and not a structural relationship.) Eventually the carpenter began to shed his responsibilities. The shipwright took over shipbuilding, and furniture was made wholly or partly by the joiner, cofferer, turner and carver, while the painter, who was also a gilder in the Middle Ages, decorated the surfaces. The upholder, or upholsterer, made cushions and mattresses and fashioned

A Charles II chest of veneered walnut on a low stand. The decorative character of this chest depends upon the use of oyster-wood veneering and cross-banding in sycamore on the edges of the panels, top and drawer. The shaped stretcher is also veneered in walnut. *Formerly in the collection of the late Robert Atkinson, F.R.I.B.A.*

Precious materials such as ivory, ebony and tortoiseshell when used as veneers were held in place by glue; like wood veneers and marquetry they were skins, which could be flayed off by adverse conditions. Many fine pieces of veneered furniture have been damaged by the high temperature and dry atmosphere of centrally-heated rooms; but gold, most precious of all materials, could be united with a surface so that it became an integral part of it, adhering like paint, but lasting much longer. The art of spreading gold over surfaces was practised in Egypt as early as the Twelfth Dynasty (2000–1788 B.C.). The metal was reduced to thin leaves by gold-beaters, and this skin, light as gossamer, could cling to a preparation of plaster. Goldbeating was known in the Graeco-Roman world and in Persia, India, China and Japan. Metal was gilded as well as pre-pared wood surfaces, and Vitruvius, in his treatise on architecture, which he dedicated to the Emperor Augustus, mentions in Book Seven that without quicksilver neither silver nor brass could be properly gilded. In Europe since the Middle Ages two distinct methods of applying gold leaf have been used: water gilding, a combination of burnished and matt finishes, and oil gilding, which cannot be burnished but is weather-resisting and may be used both on wood and iron. Nearly all the gilding on furniture was bur-nished, which was the most costly of the two processes as the wood had to be coated several times with a mixture of gilders' whitening and size, to secure a perfectly smooth and even surface. Silvering was a cheaper process, and as silvered furniture tarnished, it was sometimes protected by a coat of transparent varnish.

Gilding could lighten the effect of heavily carved features, like the massive limewood legs and scrolled frieze of the early seventeenth century Italian table, on page 39, or the eagle console table on page 158, or delicately enrich the pierced and ornamented framework of such an article as the hanging chiffonier, designed by Henry Holland and illustrated on page 8. The scroll-back, early nineteenth century chair in the King's Bedroom at the Royal Pavilion, Brighton, on page 152, is an example of the subtle emphasis gilding gave to elegant and simple lines, and the early Georgian chest from Shobdon Court, Herefordshire, on page 161, shows what an admirable ground gesso provided for the process, and the opportunities that composition gave to the carver. The sparkling contribution gilded chairs and tables made to the great salons of the eight-eenth century may be judged from the coloured plate facing page 155 of the Assembly at Wanstead House, painted by William Hogarth.

Painting as a form of decoration for furniture is probably as old as carving, and when painter and carver worked in conjunction, pictorial subjects as well as formalized orna-ment became three-dimensional, so that light and shade emphasized form and colour. Surfaces have been painted with patterns and scenes since prehistoric man adorned the walls of his cave with pictures of animals and hunting, tribal dances and magical rites, executed with virile realism in red, brown, black and several shades of yellow. Egyptian furniture was painted, sometimes with scenes of war, showing the reigning Pharaoh triumphantly pursuing his enemies, like Tutankhamen who is depicted in a chariot on one side of the small, dome-topped chest, removed from his tomb, dating from the fourteenth century B.C., and reproduced on the colour plate facing page 122. That chest is coated with a form of gesso, on which the scenes and decorative borders are painted.

36

Late seventeenth century side table with walnut veneer on a pine carcase. The flat shaped stretchers have an oval marquetry panel at the crossing point; there are inlaid panels on the drawer fronts; and the top is a fine example of floral marquetry, with walnut, ebony and other woods used in the design. Although the arrangement of the sprays and flowers is symmetrical, the individual blossoms and leaves are not, and the birds on either side of the oval panel are upside-down in relation to the central pattern. *Reproduced by courtesy of the Victoria and Albert Museum. Crown copyright.*

An English commode in the French taste, *circa* 1760-70. The carcase is pine, veneered with floral marquetry and parquetry in walnut, sycamore, box and other woods. The corner mounts, handles, escutcheon (or key plate), and the mount in the centre of the apron are of gilt-brass. From Hagley Hall, Stourbridge. *Reproduced by courtesy of the Victoria and Albert Museum. Crown copyright.*

Early seventeenth century Italian table. The stone top is veneered with red Egyptian porphyry, the legs are of limewood, carved and gilt. *Reproduced by courtesy of the Trustees of the Wallace Collection. Crown copyright.*

Gesso is also used as a ground for the painted scenes of falconry on the early fourteenth century Florentine marriage chest on page 41.

During the Middle Ages in Europe, painter and gilder were one and the same person: in England 'the king's painter' was an important Royal appointment, and, as already mentioned, Master Walter, who made the Coronation Chair, held that office under Edward I. A permanent staff of craftsmen had the fabric and furnishing of royal palaces under their care, and the chief mason, carpenter, smith and painter were as essential a part of the royal establishment as the chief butler and cook. In the castles and fortified country houses of the nobility in France, Germany and England a comparable staff of skilled craftsmen was permanently employed, and in England the office of estate carpenter and painter continued until the present century. In mediaeval houses the surface of furniture and interior woodwork was repainted regularly, for the practice of waxing and polishing wooden furniture only came in after fireplaces had replaced the open central hearth, and smoke went up a chimney instead of drifting about the room before finally escaping through louvres in the roof. After a sooty winter furniture had to be cleaned; repainting was the springtime ritual, which has come down to us as spring cleaning. The extent to which colour was used in mediaeval Europe may be judged from the fifteenth century interior opposite page 123. Vivid fabrics, glowing tapestries, painted furniture and woodwork all contributed to the rich warmth of the setting for men and women whose clothes were gorgeous though never garish.

Although the colour and marking of wood were not fully appreciated until the re-introduction of veneering, the comparatively smoke-free rooms of sixteenth and seventeenth century houses in England and France allowed wood to be left in its natural state, absolved from the annual repainting of earlier times. In Germany and Holland, where enclosed stoves tiled with porcelain had long been used, furniture and woodwork had gleamed with polish for generations. Until the seventeenth century, wood surfaces were probably treated with beeswax and turpentine, but by the end of that century, and throughout the eighteenth, spirit varnish was used, except by country makers who were faithful to traditional methods and finishes. Evelyn in *Sylva* (1664) mentions the use of linseed oil, and he obviously regarded the terms polish and varnish as interchangeable.

Painting, polishing, varnishing, japanning and lacquering were descriptive terms used after the late seventeenth century for various surface treatments and forms of decoration, and their scope should be defined. Lacquer- or lacker-work originated in the Far East, and is the art of treating the surfaces of wood or papier-mâché with the prepared sap of the lacquer tree (*Rhus vernicifera*). Many coats are applied, each rubbed down to obtain a perfectly smooth surface, and between thirty and thirty-five separate processes are necessary before the groundwork is ready for decorating. The art is ancient, and was practised in China as early as the fourth and third centuries B.C., and much later in Japan, where it developed some distinctive characteristics. Oriental lacquer imported into Europe had two main varieties of surface decoration: that on which the ornament was raised, and the other form, known as incised lacquer, with the design cut in the surface and then coloured.

The opulence of Chinese work is illustrated by the mid-eighteenth century throne of carved cinnabar-red lacquer and the black folding screen, *circa* 1722, reproduced on the coloured plate that faces page 154. A taste for Oriental art, encouraged by the seafaring nations, gradually developed in Europe, and was intermittently popular for a period of over three hundred years. After their first landing in China in 1515, the Portuguese controlled the China trade, but early in the seventeenth century their monopoly was challenged by the Dutch, who eventually captured and held the Far Eastern trade until, in turn, their monopoly was broken by the English in the eighteenth century. Lacquer-work screens and cabinets were imported in great numbers from China and Japan during the late seventeenth century, and carcases of furniture—desks, bureau-bookcases and cabinets—made chiefly in Holland, were shipped to China for lacquering, shipped back when finished, and sold at a handsome profit by Dutch merchants. Before the end of that century a European industry was established, and lacquered or japanned furniture was produced in Holland, France and England. Oriental lacquer, with its hard lustrous surface, was superior to the European substitute, which depended largely on the use of paint and varnish. But English lacquer, with its grounds of scarlet, green, blue, cream and yellow, appealed far more to Western taste than the black ground of the genuine Oriental work, and became so popular that it was

Florentine marriage chest (cassone) in walnut, with angle joints sheathed in metal, and metal strips on front and top. The surface is covered with painted gesso, depicting scenes of falconry. Early fourteenth century. *Reproduced by courtesy of the Victoria and Albert Museum. Crown copyright.*

exported to the Continent and America. An early example of English work is illustrated by the cabinet shown, closed and open, on pages 42 and 43. On the external doors, water birds and groups of figures below an exotic tree appear in high relief, executed in reds and greens on a black and gold ground; on the inside, one door is decorated by another exotic tree rising above a landscape of abrupt hills with buildings tucked away in their folds, the other by a vigorous representation of a crane—a bird that enjoyed over two hundred years of life as a decorative subject, lasting until the late nineteenth century when it was still used on Victorian folding screens. The drawer fronts in the interior display Oriental subjects seen through Western eyes, boldly drawn but lacking the delicacy and subtlety of Eastern originals. The English industry, which grew and flourished during the last quarter of the seventeenth century, was protected after 1700 by an import duty of 15 per cent on japanned and lacquered goods from the Far East. The publication, in 1688, of *A Treatise of Japaning and Varnishing*, by John Stalker and George Parker, had done much to popularize the new craft of 'japanning', and that term thereafter applied not only to lacquer-work but to painted and varnished furniture generally. Lacquer was also adopted as a general term for transparent or opaque varnishes, and for the brilliant translucent varnish perfected and patented early in the eighteenth century by a French family of artist-craftsmen named Martin which became known all over Europe as *vernis martin*. By the middle of the century the brothers Martin—Guillaume, Simon Étienne, Julien and Robert—were directing at least three lacquer-producing factories in Paris which were classed, in 1748, as a 'manufacture nationale'. Bailey's *Dictionarium Britannicum* (second edition, 1736) describes *lacker* as

41

*Above and opposite :* Cabinet japanned in gold, silver, red and green with a black ground, on a stand of carved and silvered pinewood. English: last quarter of the seventeenth century. The gilt-brass mounts and the drawer handles are not original. The decorative subjects are executed with spirit, but they lack the delicacy of Oriental work. The florid carving of the stand is so robust that the figures, emerging from a froth of scrollwork are positively bloated. Such emphatic, and indeed heavy-handed, carved work was characteristic of the elaborate cabinet stands of the Carolean period. *Reproduced by courtesy of the Victoria and Albert Museum. Crown copyright.*

*Above, left:* **Dining room sideboard designed by Charles Lock Eastlake, who advocated the hand polishing of wood and condemned French polishing, staining or varnishing. Reproduced on a reduced scale from plate XII of his** *Hints on Household Taste* **(second edition, 1869).**

*Above, right:* **Oak sideboard, carved and inlaid with ebony, sycamore, and bleached mahogany. Designed by William Richard Lethaby about 1900 for Melsetter House, Hoy, Orkney Islands. Lethaby had a sense of style, which Eastlake lacked completely, and this sideboard is typical of the best work of the designers and artist-craftsmen who continued the Arts and Crafts movement that William Morris had inspired.** *Reproduced by courtesy of the Victoria and Albert Museum. Crown copyright.*

*Right:* **An early nineteenth century oak dresser from the Swansea Valley. The craftsman who made this was working in a living tradition: craft revivals by gifted amateurs were still half a century ahead.** *Reproduced by permission of the National Museum of Wales. Welsh Folk Museum.*

44

*Above:* Cabinet designed by Philip Webb, and painted by William Morris with scenes from the story of St George, 1861.

*Left:* Carved walnut cabinet, inlaid with various woods, with six enamel panels inset and three metal relief panels illustrating 'The Sleeping Beauty'. Designed by Bruce Talbert, the author of *Gothic Forms Applied to Furniture*. This cabinet, made by Holland and Sons, was shown at the International Exhibition, Paris, 1867.
*Both subjects reproduced by courtesy of the Victoria and Albert Museum. Crown copyright.*

Chest covered with embroidery in wool and silk cross-stitch, on a walnut stand with decorative twist turning on the legs. French: late seventeenth century. *Reproduced by courtesy of the Victoria and Albert Museum. Crown copyright.*

'a varnish used over leaf silver, in gilding picture frames'. The coating of polished metal surfaces with varnish to prevent discolouration was also known as lacquering.

The authors of *A Treatise of Japaning and Varnishing* stated that a shellac spirit varnish was used for polishing both the best and lower grades of furniture, with many more coats applied to the former. After the application of each coat, the spirits evaporated, leaving a thin film of shellac on the surface. When the surface had been built up by ten or twelve coats, it was given a high polish with a mineral substance called tripoli, that formerly came from North Africa. Only two or three coats of a poorer quality of shellac were given to the lower grade furniture, and polishing was omitted. French polishing, a much later invention, was introduced probably towards the close of the eighteenth century, though not adopted by English cabinet-makers until the 1820s. Sometimes described as friction varnishing, this process consisted of thickly coating a surface with transparent gum, which gave a highly glazed effect to the colour and figure of wood without the need for prolonged polishing. By the middle of the nineteenth century, French polishing in conjunction with stains had led to the obliteration of the real colour of wood. In *The Cabinet-Maker's Guide*, by G. A. Siddons, which had reached its fifth edition in 1830, instructions were given for staining beech a mahogany colour, and imitating rosewood, kingwood, and staining horn in imitation of tortoiseshell. 'Staining,' said the author, 'is chiefly in use among chair-makers, and when properly conducted and varnished, has a most beautiful appearance, and is less likely to meet with injury than japanning.' Charles Lock Eastlake, an English architect and furniture designer writing in the 1860s, condemned all such processes. 'The present system of French-polishing,' he said, 'or literally *varnishing*, furniture is destructive of all artistic effect in its appearance, because the surface of wood thus lacquered can never change its colour, or acquire that rich hue which is one of the charms of old cabinet-work.' (See page 44.) Before the introduction of French polishing, wood surfaces had everything to gain from the passage of time; elbow grease expended by generations of servants and housewives deepened and enriched the natural tone of oak, walnut, mahogany, elm, yew, cherry and apple; but once wood had been stained and French-polished its hue was unalterable, unfading evidence of the manufacturer's often deplorable taste in colour.

Finishes that disguised wood, and allowed a humble and inexpensive material like beech to masquerade as mahogany, or something more rare and exotic, became increasingly popular during the forty years between 1825 and 1865, when furniture-making was changing from a craft to a largely mechanized industry. Few countries apart from Scandinavia accomplished that transition gracefully, and in England one article alone, the Windsor chair, escaped unscathed in form. In rebellion against debased design, flimsy construction, and deceitful finishes, William Morris (1834–96), poet, social reformer, and gifted artist-craftsman, attempted to revive handicrafts that were threatened with extinction, and his revolt against industrial methods and his personal genius as a designer inspired the Arts and Crafts movement, which aroused interest in simple, well-made furniture and the natural beauty of wood as a material. That new interest was given rapid and practical expression in the Scandinavian countries, and the teaching and work of Morris were taken far more seriously in Europe than in his own country, where his ideas appealed only to a small though influential élite. Few people were sufficiently enlightened or sufficiently wealthy to buy hand-made furniture, but there was enough effective patronage to encourage many artist-craftsmen who, during the last thirty years of the nineteenth century and the opening decades of the twentieth, produced some fine examples of furniture, original in conception and very obviously English in character, like the sideboard on page 44, made about 1900 to the design of William Richard Lethaby (1857–1931). This high-backed piece, with its arcaded shelves and flanking cupboards, is of oak, carved and inlaid with ebony, sycamore and bleached mahogany. It resembles the traditional dresser form, rather than the more compact sideboard of the late eighteenth century, and should be compared with the far more sophisticated examples designed nearly thirty years later by Gordon Russell and reproduced on pages 6 and 189. The reappraisal of wood as an intrinsically decorative material followed the work and example of designers and artist-craftsmen like Ernest Gimson (1864–1919) and Ambrose Heal (1872–1959) in England, Karl Malmsten in Sweden, and Léon Jallot, René Joubert and Jacques Ruhlmann in France. The cumulative effect of a revived interest in the colour and marking of wood is demonstrated by the 'contemporary' style of furniture that has developed during and since the 1950s in Britain, the United States and many European countries. The surfaces on most examples of this furniture, though left unstained and in a natural colour, are protected by a hard, transparent lacquer varnish, which, like French polish, does not allow wood to acquire the mature richness of tone conferred by time. By rejecting this gift we are back where we were when Eastlake criticized staining and French polishing a century ago.

So far we have described methods of decoration that depend on inlaying or treating the surface of wood with substances that are partly absorbed by it, or which adhere as a skin, excessively thin, as in gilding, or more substantial, as in the various forms of veneering; but a far older technique was to cover wooden frames or surfaces with leather or fabrics. Leather-covered chairs, stools, beds and cushions were used as early as the Old Kingdom of Ancient Egypt, 2980–2475 B.C., and methods of treating the hides and skins of various animals to make them flexible for clothes and furniture are probably older still. In the Middle Ages, long before the revival of veneering, the coffer-maker or cofferer was covering chests and chair frames with leather. Coffer-maker's chairs were generally made of beech with an X-shaped frame, like the example opposite and from this open frame a seat of webbing and canvas was slung on which a cushion rested. The back uprights ended in finials or pommels, carved and gilded, sometimes enamelled, or simply terminating in balls as on the chair from the fifteenth century manuscript, reproduced on page 91. By the early seventeenth century such X-shaped chairs had become broader in the seat, far more luxurious, completely covered with velvet, including the finials, and decorated with brass-headed or gilt round-topped nails. The contemporary term for this form of decoration was 'garnished with nails', and it was applied to leather-covered chests and trunks as well as chairs. The late seventeenth century English chest with two drawers in the lower part, shown on page 108, is patterned with brass nails which form the monogram of William and Mary on the lid.

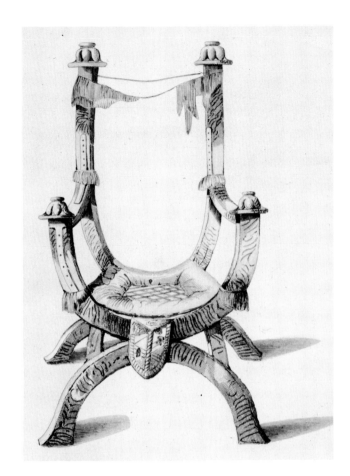

Coffer-maker's chair, with the frame originally covered in fabric and leather, preserved in the vestry of York Minster. Such chairs, apparently copied from Flemish models, were made in England during the late fifteenth and early sixteenth centuries. Reproduced from plate VI of Shaw's *Specimens of Ancient Furniture*.

Leather was stamped and embossed with patterns, painted and gilded, and used for hangings, for folding screens, for chair backs and seats, and in the eighteenth century by cabinet-makers on the tops of library and writing tables and desks. For that purpose the material was dyed, usually a deep red, green or blue, and had delicately tooled gilded borders. Decorated leather was used throughout Europe during the Middle Ages, and the best of it came from Spain, where the tradition of skilled leather working established in the Moorish kingdom of Cordova long survived.

Leather was not the only material used for close-covering furniture, for the mediaeval upholsterer had employed that technique on beds. The selour or celure (the contemporary name for the head) and the tester (or canopy) were richly clothed, and an account of the furnishing of the bedroom prepared for the Lorde Grautehuse, the envoy of Charles, Duke of Burgundy, who was entertained in 1472 by Edward IV, mentions 'the Counterpoynte clothe of golde . . . the Tester and the Celer also shyninge clothe of golde . . .' During the sixteenth century, the fashion for monumental bedsteads of wood, with elaborately carved columns and testers, restricted the upholsterer's work to curtains, mattress, pillows and counterpane; but by the end of the following century and during the early years of the eighteenth, the tall state beds in royal palaces and great houses had posts, head and canopy covered in the same material as the curtains. The direct application of fabrics to flat, curved, or carved surfaces was a highly specialized part of the upholsterer's craft, and small boxes, desks and chests were often close-covered with damask, brocatelle or embroidery in coloured silks and wools, like the French chest on page 46.

The term upholstery, while embracing the general use of fabrics in furnishing and the manufacture of beds and bedding, became specifically related to the padding, stuffing, and covering of seat furniture. As early as the fifteenth century, padding was fixed to chair seats, and improvements in the technique of upholstery came two hundred years later, when both seats and backs were padded. The skill and inventiveness of upholsterers progressively increased comfort between the late seventeenth century and the first half of the nineteenth, when coiled springs came into general use for mattresses, easy chairs and other upholstered furniture. Before spring upholstery established our modern standard of comfort, padding on the seat, arms and back of chairs had been made soft and yielding with fillings of wool, hair, and oddments of waste fabric.

Covering materials were richly varied. Velvet, a silken textile with a very close piled surface, which probably originated in the Far East, was made in Italy and known in the fourteenth century, when Chaucer described its softness in *The Romaunt of the Rose* in this couplet:

> 'Sprang up the gras, as thikke y-set
> And softe as any velüet. . . .'

Brocade was a finely woven silk fabric, with one or more colours added that appeared on the face of the material. Brocatelle, or brocatel, was an imitation of brocade, in coarse silk or cotton, with a raised design in the warp and a plain weft background. (Warp is the term for threads stretched lengthwise in a loom, while threads woven into and crossing the warp are known as the weft or woof.) Mohair, or mohaire, a cloth made from the wool of the Angora goat, was used occasionally for upholstery after the late seventeenth century, also moreen, or morine, a strong woollen material sometimes mixed with cotton. Moreen was a cheap imitation of moiré, a silken cloth with a closely woven rib, highly lustrous surface, and a watered figure, that was used in the eighteenth century for bed curtains. Satin was of Chinese origin, probably taking its name from the port of Zayton, a place mentioned by Marco Polo and famous for the manufacture of a rich silk textile. Zettani was the mediaeval Italian name for this luxurious material. In *The Book of the Duchesse*, Chaucer describes a feather bed,

> 'Rayed with golde, and right wel cled
> In fyn black satin. . . .'

Satin was originally made of silk, with a sheen on the smooth surface, usually woven with the warp forming the face, and the weave so close that its structure was imperceptible in the finished cloth.

The view of the north drawing-room at Ham House opposite, shows the sumptuous effect of rich fabrics in association with carved and gilded and painted furniture in the

The north drawing-room at Ham House, Surrey. The armchairs standing against the walls have painted and gilt frames, upholstered in crimson velvet with gold braid borders: the chairs at each side of the table have carved and gilt frames, the feet representing the heads of dolphins, a device that also terminates the arms of the elbow chair: both are upholstered in brocaded satin. The partly gilded walnut table in the centre with legs in the form of caryatids, is probably the work of the Dutch craftsmen who worked in the employ of the Duke and Duchess of Lauderdale at Ham House between 1673 and 1679. *Reproduced by courtesy of the Victoria and Albert Museum. Crown copyright.*

latter part of the seventeenth century. The armchairs ranged against the walls have painted and gilt frames, upholstered in crimson velvet with gold braid borders; the brocaded satin chairs with the dolphins carved on the feet are part of a set of twelve. The English tapestries on the walls, woven in silk and wool by former Mortlake weavers, may be dated between 1699 and 1719. A seventeenth century Persian carpet covers the floor. In that drawing-room the furnishing and interior decoration combine to create an atmosphere of exuberant luxury, not in the sense of cushioned comfort, but visual luxury; everywhere the eye is held and delighted by some ornamental expression of sheer high spirits, whether conveyed by the partly gilded walnut table with its carved caryatids, the florid gilded plasterwork of the chimneypiece, or the warm richness of the upholstered chairs. The unity of design between furniture and background in the Kent interior at Wanstead house is not apparent here; though furniture and background have characteristics in common. Large rooms of the same period in France were designed so that furniture and wall treatment were closely related in design, an orderly relationship strengthened by the suite, which became fashionable during the seventeenth century and consisted of chairs, stools and couches, sometimes as many as twenty-four chairs and stools and two or four couches.

To all these richly furnished rooms needlework contributed even more colour and variety than such materials as velvet and brocade. Celia Fiennes has left an account of a house at Epsom that she visited at some time between 1701 and 1703. 'You enter one room hung with crosstitch in silks,' she noted, 'the bed the same lined with yellow and white strip'd satin, window curtains white silk damaske with furbellows of callicoe printed flowers, the chaires crosstitch, and two stooles of yellow mohaire with crostitch true lover knots in straps along and a cross, an elbow chaire tentstitch, glasses over all the chimneys and marble pieces; the windows in all the roomes has cusheons. . . .' By that she meant cushioned window seats. Cross-stitch was the term for two stitches crossing each other at right angles, and *gros-point* was a form of cross-stitch embroidery in wool on canvas. Coloured wools and silks are used in cross-stitches for the embroidery that covers the chest on page 46. *Gros-point*, used extensively for upholstery, was coarser and more rigid than *petit-point*, which was a form of fine embroidery worked upon fine-meshed canvas, that was usually held in a frame during the work. Tent-stitch, the finest of all embroidery stitches, was nearly always used in *petit-point* and gave a closely and evenly filled hard-wearing surface, especially suitable for seat furniture. Tent-stitch enabled the embroiderer to use highly detailed pictorial subjects, and the stitch was worked diagonally over single vertical and horizontal threads of the canvas, giving a smooth and even effect, the same both sides. On many needlework chair and settee coverings, both *gros-point* and *petit-point* are used, as on the example opposite of a high-backed winged arm-chair in walnut. A type of surface decoration on fabrics, known as appliqué, consists of shaped pieces of material applied to form a pattern. Each separate piece is cut out, the edges turned in and stitched down before being arranged in the design, and finally secured to the ground material by an embroidery stitch, or with braid or cord round the edges; occasionally the work is enriched by embroidery between the applied parts of the design.

52

English winged arm-chair, *circa* **1700**, with walnut frame, upholstered in *gros-point* and *petit-point* embroidery. *Reproduced by courtesy of the Victoria and Albert Museum. Crown copyright.*

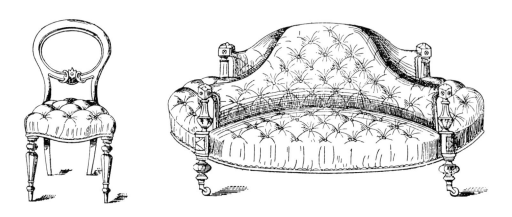

Examples of mid-nineteenth century buttoned upholstery.
*Left :* **A balloon-back mahogany single chair.**
*Right :* **A circular ottoman, divided into four seats. From a trade catalogue by an unknown maker,** *circa* **1840-45.**

During the second half of the eighteenth century the surface of upholstered work was varied ornamentally by buttoning, which was used both by chair-makers and coach-builders. Beginning as a purely decorative device, buttoning was soon recognized as a practical method of securing a hard-wearing, resilient surface, and became increasingly popular throughout the nineteenth century; it is occasionally used today by contemporary designers. Stitches of strong thread drew the thick padding and outer cover of an upholstered seat or back into a form of quilting, producing either a moderately varied or a corpulently bulging surface. The stitches were concealed by buttons or rosettes, arranged in neat rows or in squares, diamonds or half-diamonds. Coach-builders always called this technique quilting, and used it for the interior lining of every type of vehicle from sedan chairs to stage coaches, and from the earliest days of railway travel it was adopted for first class compartments. The over-emphasis of the technique is illustrated by the balloon-back Victorian chair shown above.

A material that competed with upholstery was woven canework, introduced to Europe and England from India and China in the second half of the seventeenth century. This was much finer than anything produced by basketmakers, and consisted of canes split into thin strips and interwoven to form an openwork mesh; the material was provided by the class of palms known as rattan or calamus, and was used originally in a large mesh, but before the end of the seventeenth century a closer mesh was favoured. Despite the protests of upholsterers and the woollen trade, cane chair-makers had established themselves as a flourishing branch of the English furniture industry by the opening of the eighteenth century, and although canework never replaced elaborate textiles and needlework, it provided a yielding and resilient surface for the seats and backs of chairs, day-beds and settees, and allowed light-framed sets of chairs to be produced very cheaply in large numbers. Although it went out of fashion periodically, canework was always reintroduced either for its decorative character, its comfort, or both, and in the latter part of the nineteenth century the all-canework lounge chair, based on an Indian design, became exceedingly popular.

Of all the many ways of decorating furniture, the oldest is almost certainly carving, for palaeolithic man with a flint burin could incise drawings and patterns on bone. For over five thousand years skill in carving has developed, risen to high standards of accomplishment, declined, and started up again from primitive beginnings. The simplest form is known as scratch carving, consisting of single lines incised or scratched on the surface of woodwork, and found only on furniture made in the countryside, though seldom later than the early eighteenth century. (The incised decoration on the back of the joined chair on page 16 is an advanced form of scratch carving.) Gouge work, or gouge carving, is another relatively simple form of decoration, consisting of regularly spaced shallow depressions, scooped out with a gouge. This was used extensively in the last half of the sixteenth and throughout the seventeenth centuries. Chip carving, though earlier and more ambitious, was used on mediaeval chests. The patterns, usually in the form of roundels, were first set out with compasses and chalk, then chipped out with a sharp tool, most probably by the joiner who made the chest. This was not ornament in relief, raised above the surface by cutting away the background; nor was it as boldly three-dimensional as sculpture in wood or stone; that kind of wood-carving required more dexterity than the mediaeval joiner could command, but even such a simple technique as chip carving could produce an almost dazzling decorative effect, as illustrated by the chest on page 81, which is ornamented with crisp, decisive geometrical patterns. Such relatively simple techniques as chip carving and gouge work were suggested by the tools the joiner used in his constructional work; decoration was incidental, a bit of fun that livened up surfaces, and while it remained in that elementary stage, it was a happy relaxation for the craftsman who made joined chests and chairs. The highly skilled professional wood-carver, a craftsman in his own right, well established in the Middle Ages, had by the seventeenth century asserted his claim to be recognized as independent of cabinet-makers and chair-makers, and, as mentioned in the previous chapter, went into partnership with the gilder and became a designer and maker of decorative furniture. Some of the results of that collaboration are shown by the table on page 39, the cabinet stand on pages 42 and 43, the table and chairs at Ham House on page 51, and the mirror frames on pages 132 and 133.

Carving is a natural and obvious way of decorating furniture, either by cutting patterns, piercing surfaces, or shaping such members as chair and table legs. Piercing was probably utilitarian in origin, used to ventilate cupboards where food was kept, developing in time from crude punctures in a door panel, to ornamental patterns cut with a fretsaw and applied to surfaces or adorning the edges of tables or shelves with delicate galleries, like those on the gilt chiffonier on page 8. Moulding, another method of shaping wood, differs from carving, and in addition to performing a structural function, is used to modify the sharp edges of table tops, chair-seats and arms, bedposts and the angles of case furniture. Mouldings are also used to give surface variation to flat expanses of woodwork, as for example on the panels of the Dutch built-in oak bedstead that faces page 1, or the doors of the English mahogany press on page 29; but apart from satisfying the eye, by bringing a well-finished look to furniture, mouldings also satisfy the sense of touch by softening abrupt angles. The simplest form of moulding is that struck or scratched directly on solid members, such as the stiles and rails on the early seventeenth century English oak chest on page 13. There are struck mouldings

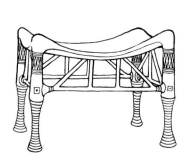

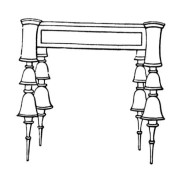

*Above, left*: Ancient Egyptian stool with ring-turned legs.
*Centre*: **Greek chair with turned legs, from the Parthenon frieze, fifth century B.C. (See page 66.)**
*Right*: **Roman stool from Herculaneum, with bell-turned legs. Such stools, cast in bronze, were derived from a wooden prototype. From Trollope's** *Illustrations of Ancient Art.*

*Right*: **A faldestool, or chair of state, with ball and ring turning. First half of twelfth century A.D. Drawn by F. W. Fairholt from an illuminated manuscript of the Psalms in the library of Trinity College, Cambridge. Reproduced from** *A History of Domestic Manners and Sentiments in England,* **by Thomas Wright (1862).**

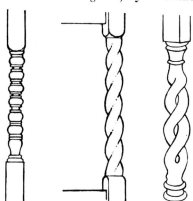

**Three examples of late seventeenth century decorative turning.**
*Left*: **Bobbin.**
*Centre*: **Double twist (the so-called 'barley sugar' twist).**
*Right*: **Double open twist.**

on the underside of the top rail and the inner sides of the stiles: the muntins and the bottom rail are chamfered, by planing off the edges, to give a flat, inclined surface instead of a right angle. ('Stuck' moulding is a corruption of the original term.) During the sixteenth and seventeenth centuries, the purely ornamental practice was introduced of making mouldings separately and applying them to chests, cupboards and drawers. This gave a play of light and shade to surfaces, but with the increase of veneering the fashion for heavy applied mouldings diminished in popularity, though bolection mouldings were used to cover the joints between two members with surfaces at different levels and to project beyond them. Carvers enriched mouldings with ornament, but the character of such enrichment and the proportions of mouldings are subjects for the next chapter.

The technique of turning invited experiments in decoration, and the lathe made it easy for simple forms of ornament to be repeated. The rings or annulets cut on the haft

56

of an axe or a club, to improve the grip, may have suggested the earliest type of turned ornament; but the decorative possibilities of the technique were soon realized in the Ancient World, and employed by furniture-makers with ingenuity and elegance. The Egyptians used precise and delicate outlines for the turned legs of stools and chairs; they elaborated turning, and, not content with plain cylindrical shafts, gave them a concave outline, decorated throughout their length with rings set close together. Turned cones, ornamented with scales, terminated the legs of Assyrian stools and thrones; ball turning adorned the framing of Greek chairs; bell and ring turning the legs of Etruscan and Roman seats and tables. The Romano-British sepulchral monument on page 70 includes a couch with legs turned in the form of balusters; another example of the same period on page 18, depicts a table with slightly concave undecorated turned legs.

Mediaeval turners used simple forms of ball and ring turning, like the examples opposite, or rings only, as on the legs and stretchers of the fifteenth century basin stand on page 78. Something inspired turners to become experimental and inventive in the mid-seventeenth century, particularly in England and the American colonies of New England; this sudden desire to explore new ways of ornamenting turned work may have been stimulated by Puritan repression, for throughout the Commonwealth period luxurious and highly decorative furniture was disliked by the glum dictators who took the colour out of English life. The decline of the luxury trades turned the attention of furniture-makers to the possibilities of restoring a little gaiety by ornamenting the frames of chairs and tables; turners evolved lively variations of ball and bobbin and ring turning, and presently carvers introduced the spiral twist and later, after the Puritan dictatorship ended, the double twist or double rope, which resembled a stick of barley sugar. (The term 'barley-sugar twist' is not contemporary, for although that sweetmeat was probably made early in the eighteenth century, the first record of its name so far discovered is in 1789 in a book called *The Complete Confectioner*.)

Open twist was another form of spiral ornament, known as double twist when there were two members, and triple when there were three. Open and 'barley-sugar' varieties are shown opposite, and examples of late seventeenth century forms are illustrated by the English and Indo-Dutch chairs on pages 120 and 121, the legs of the table on page 37 and the stand on page 46. The device was not confined to legs and the backs and arm supports of chairs; it also appeared on the hoods of long-case clocks and the fronts of cabinets. The spiral twist was derived from an architectural prototype, for it was used in Romanesque work of the eleventh and twelfth centuries, and far more impressively by Renaissance architects in such magnificent compositions as the baldacchino at St Peter's, Rome, designed by Bernini with four colossal twisted columns supporting the great bronze canopy. The twist as an ornamental form was fully developed in Italy, France, Spain, Switzerland, Germany and Holland before it was introduced to England, and as such work was carved by hand the comparatively simple corkscrew form was often elaborated almost beyond recognition. Modern lathes have a special attachment which enables twisted work to be turned mechanically; but the early work was hand wrought.

# CHAPTER FOUR

# The Mediaeval Scene

DURING the dark ages that followed the end of the Western Roman Empire in 476, the refinements and luxuries of life became memories throughout large areas of Europe, and disappeared completely from Britain, where prosperous towns declined and great country estates and their well-appointed houses were abandoned. The Teutonic barbarians who settled in the former provinces of the Empire were warriors, pirates and professional looters, but they were not wholly ignorant of the crafts and were competent carpenters and shipwrights. They were able to build timber-framed halls and to furnish them with such simple articles as benches and tables, strongly though crudely made. Creative opportunity for design in architecture and the ancillary arts survived only in Constantinople and some of the cities of the Middle East and Egypt; but until mediaeval civilization slowly emerged, and imposed the image of Christian unity on the patchwork of European states, the arts were neglected, and many crafts were dedicated solely to military needs. Even when United Christendom was recognized by kings and princes and powerful landlords, the barbaric habits and standards of earlier ages persisted; art and learning flourished only in the great religious establishments, and elsewhere, during the twelfth and thirteenth centuries, furniture remained at a stage of primitive utility.

Early inventories and wills, of which many survive, disclose how scantily homes were furnished; even wealthy citizens owned little besides a trestle table, with boards that could stand in a corner or against a wall except at meal times, a few benches and three-legged stools, for chairs were a rarity, and in the richest houses there was seldom more than one, which was used exclusively by the master of the household, not an easy chair, but something massive and stately, too heavy to be moved about and usually kept in the same place. As mentioned in chapter one, basketwork chairs were almost

*Right, above:* **A trestle table and a low bench: fifteenth century. MS. Can. Lit. 99. fol. 6. R. Bodleian Library.**

*Right, below:* **A table dormante, with a free-standing low-backed settle. Drawn by F. W. Fairholt from the fifteenth century illuminated manuscript,** *Roman de la Violette.* **Reproduced from** *A History of Domestic Manners and Sentiments in England,* **by Thomas Wright (1862).**

certainly in common use; but they had no more social prestige than a three-legged stool. Flat-topped chests were used for seats, ranged along a wall with strips of fabric on their lids. By the mid-fourteenth century, the ancestral types of nearly all our present-day articles of furniture had appeared, but for generations they retained an elementary simplicity of form, like the trestle table and the low bench at the top of this page. The lower illustration shows an advance in comfort and convenience: a settle with a low back stands before a table dormant (sometimes spelt dormante), a permanent or fixed side table, indicative of wealth and hospitality, as suggested by Chaucer when describing the open-handed affluence of the Frankeleyn, in the Prologue of *The Canterbury Tales.* His account of the abundance of food and drink always available concludes with the lines:

'His table dormant in his halle alway
Stood redy covered al the longe day.'

The tables in both illustrations have table-cloths, items that appeared in many

*Left:* A royal card party, from the MS. of the romance of *Meliadus*, written in France between the years 1330 and 1350.

*Right:* A circular card table, from an illuminated MS. of the early fifteenth century, possibly of Flemish origin. Both subjects drawn from the original MSS. by F. W. Fairholt and included in Thomas Wright's *The Homes of Other Days* (1871).

contemporary inventories, for only servants ate off the bare boards. From the Middle Ages until the eighteenth century the top of the table, the board, was always thought of as something separate and distinct from the supporting structure; the word table meant the top only; legs and rails were called the frame; and the complete article was known as a table with frame. The term table dormant was still current in the first half of the seventeenth century, and an inventory of 1638 includes 'One planke Table with the Dormants. . . .' Table, derived from the Latin *tabula*, a board, was used concurrently with the old English word board as early as the fourteenth century, and in the sixteenth century they were sometimes used together as table-board. A mediaeval game called tables, apparently a form of backgammon, is mentioned by Chaucer in 'The Frankeleyns Tale' (line 900):

'They dauncen, and they pleyen at ches and tables . . .'

Over two centuries later it was still popular, and Shakespeare in *Love's Labour Lost* (Act V, Scene 2), wrote:

'This is the ape of form, monsieur the nice,
That, when he plays at tables, chides the dice
In honourable terms. . . .'

The hinged boards known as 'a pair of tables' may have originated in the double board used for the game. Playing cards were introduced in the fourteenth century, and two card parties are shown above in Fairholt's drawings, made from contemporary illuminated manuscripts. The circular table, supported by a central pillar, may have been specially designed for card playing. A record dated 1529 appears to refer to card tables as specialized articles of furniture, for it reads: '. . . for avoydinge of dyce and carde

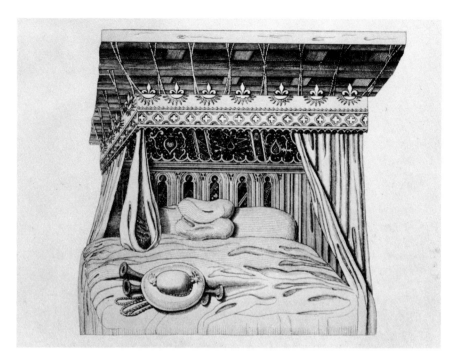

*Above, left*: **A fifteenth century bed with the canopy suspended from the ceiling beams. From the French MS.** *des Miracles de Saint Louis,* **reproduced in Shaw's** *Specimens of Ancient Furniture.*

*Above, right*: **Fifteenth century bedroom interior, showing the draped bed, a high-backed chair with a canopy, and a three-legged turned wash-stand and bowl. MS. Douce 208, fol. I. n. Bodleian Library.**

tables and all other unlawful gamys which were then by commandement prohybett. . . .' But the reference could be to the game of tables. Another use of the word is probably derived from the French *tableau*, for in an inventory of Henry VIII, table sometimes meant a painting on a panel, a framed painting, or framed carvings, enamels or needle-work, when hung on a wall.

The lavish use of decorative hangings and fabrics in mediaeval interiors is illustrated by the coloured plate opposite page 123; in wealthy households tapestries adorned the walls, in bedrooms heavy curtains hung from bed canopies, while on the yielding feather beds, valuable quilts and rich materials were spread. As no easy chairs existed, even kings and popes would often sit on their beds to receive ambassadors; and such audiences held in royal or papal bedchambers certainly allowed the chief performer to be far more comfortable than he could be on a flat-seated, high-backed throne or chair of state.

Originally the word bed probably meant the materials upon which people slept, and it is apparently used in that sense by Chaucer in 'The Reves Tale', when he describes the making of a temporary bed for some guests:

> 'And in his own chambre hem made a bed
> With shetes and with chalons faire y-spred . . .'

78

Chalons was the mediaeval name for woollen coverlets or blankets, after Châlons-sur-Marne in France, where the material was first made. Chaucer's description of the rich materials used on beds has been quoted in chapter two (page 50), and the illustrations opposite suggest how luxurious a bed could be, though the furnishing of the bedroom on the right is sparse. Both the beds shown have testers from which the curtains hang; and the tester is suspended from the ceiling in the example on the left, with a decorative valance concealing the top of the curtains, and a wood celure, or bed-head, carved with cusped arches. Apart from the bed, two articles only appear in the bedroom: the high-backed seat with a canopy, which is really a state chair, and the wash-stand in the foreground, with three turned legs and stretchers, supporting a basin, slightly more generous in size than basin stands used in the eighteenth century. (See page 143.)

The Gothic canopy and pinnacles of that state chair, and the cusped arches of the bed-head, suggest how furniture was related to contemporary architectural design; a relationship that grew more marked as furniture became increasingly decorative. When describing the Coronation Chair in chapter two, we said that Gothic forms could appear equally well in stone, metal or wood, for master craftsmen could handle all materials. Although the craft guilds regulated the scope of work done by their members, and were vigilant about the maintenance of high standards of execution, many skills were complementary and sometimes interchangeable, and all skilled men worked within the framework of a living and developing architectural tradition. In the fifteenth and early sixteenth centuries the carved decoration that enriched the work of joiners had the delicacy and vitality of the last phase of Gothic architecture in Europe and England. The panels of the French chest on page 83, and the mid-fifteenth century oak chair on page 86, that was formerly the right-hand seat of a triple throne on the dais of the Great Hall in St Mary's Guildhall at Coventry, display the characteristic forms of Gothic tracery carved on a solid wooden surface, what is known as 'blind' tracery, while pierced tracery decorates the back panels and doors of the plate cupboard and aumbry on page 84, and the oak food cupboard on page 85 is pierced and carved with tracery, a crocketed gable, and a feather device. Woodcarvers also evolved their own individual forms of decoration, and of these a stylized representation of linen arranged in vertical folds was the most popular. This linen-fold pattern was invented, probably by Flemish carvers, late in the fifteenth century, and soon appeared with regional versions in France, Germany and England. Perhaps it was used originally on linen chests and cupboards or receptacles where documents were kept, for the vertical mouldings, ending in folds, also resembled scrolls of parchment. Linenfold, or parchment panels, as they are sometimes called, decorated walls as well as furniture, and examples of English and French variations are shown on the two seats on page 90. The device had no architectural prototype, nor was it akin in any way to carvers' work in stone, like the geometrical roundels ornamenting the boarded chest on page 81.

Heraldic devices played a conspicuous part in the appearance of later mediaeval furniture, for the science of heraldry in the fourteenth and fifteenth centuries was more widely understood in that illiterate age than the alphabet. What began as a relatively simple code of distinguishing marks painted on shields to allow men in armour to tell

*Above:* Thirteenth century dug-out chest, from Orleton Church, Herefordshire. The most elementary form of receptacle, scooped from a roughly squared-up tree trunk, and fitted with a lid.

*Below:* Iron-bound thirteenth century chest from Kingstone, Herefordshire: a larger example of the dug-out type.

*Both subjects reproduced from H.M. Inventory of the Royal Commission on Historical Monuments, Herefordshire. By permission of the Controller of H.M. Stationery Office. Crown Copyright.*

friend from foe in the height of battle, developed into a highly decorative legible language for proclaiming status or ownership, that was used not only by royal and noble families, but by such collective bodies as guilds, trade associations, and city governments. Various hues, known as tinctures, were classified as *metals, colours,* and *furs,* and appeared on shields and their bearings; from these tinctures and the shape of the lines separating them when more than one was used, and from a great range of symbols, a graphic glossary was built up. Those symbols, carved in wood or on stone, cast in plaster or painted on glass, included formalized representations of birds, beasts and fishes, variations on such classic hybrids as the griffin and harpy, fabulous creatures like the wyvern, unicorn, cockatrice, and dragon, also trees, flowers, wreaths, and such inanimate objects as crowns, turbans, ships, shoes, chains, keys, towers, turrets, battlements, and gates.

Thirteenth century boarded chest of oak, decorated with chip-carved roundels. English: said to have come from a church in Hampshire. Compare with the boarded chest of the same period on page 11. *Reproduced by courtesy of the Victoria and Albert Museum. Crown copyright.*

Such symbols, never used purely as decorative motifs, were carved or painted to convey a meaning and establish an identity. What they contributed to richness of texture and liveliness of colour was incidentally, not intentionally decorative.

Between the middle of the fourteenth century and the beginning of the sixteenth, such basic articles of furniture as beds, tables, chests, cupboards and seats were improved in structure and design. Mediaeval furniture, whether made in France, Flanders, Germany or England, had a comparable simplicity of form, differing only in the character and execution of ornament. In Spain and Italy the shape of furniture had greater elegance and the decoration greater liveliness than in Northern and Central Europe, for the oriental Moorish states of Spain, though shrinking in size, still wielded a potent artistic influence, and in Italy classic traditions of design, though submerged, were never far below the surface. Progress in design was slow, because furniture lasted far longer than a lifetime, and oak chests as massive as those shown opposite and above survived in constant use for generations. In the Middle Ages, chests and coffers were the most important items in furnishing, for they housed clothes and valuables.

The coffer was essentially a portable receptacle, the ancestor of the travelling trunk, varying in size from a large dome-topped wooden box, covered with leather and banded with iron, to a small money chest like the example on the table illustrated at the top of page 88. When used for travelling, the larger types were called trussing coffers, the word trussing being used in the old sense of packing. One item in a will made by Roger de Kyrby, Perpetual Vicar of Gaynford, and dated 1412, is: 'a pair of trussyngcofers,

The Great Hall, Penshurst Place, Kent, perhaps the finest example of a mediaeval hall. The building dates from 1341; the screens were put in during the latter part of the sixteenth century, and include some modern work; and the long tables and benches down each side are fifteenth century. This was the characteristic Gothic interior, with tracery in the windows and a fine timber roof, with beams darkened by smoke from the central hearth on its way out through the louvres. When people no longer lived or sat 'round the fire', and the central hearth was supplanted by the wall fireplace, the arrangement and character of furnishing changed, the communal life of the great hall survived only in the spacious kitchens of large farm houses, and wealthy noblemen and merchants enjoyed greater privacy. *Copyright: 'Country Life'.*

*Above:* Carved oak Gothic chest, French, late fifteenth century. The influence of contemporary architecture is obvious. *Reproduced by courtesy of the Victoria and Albert Museum.*

*Left:* Detail of West Front, Sens Cathedral, *circa* 1490. The tracery of the circular window and the 'blind' tracery carved on the chest are comparable examples of the last, the *Tertiaire*, or *Flamboyant*, phase of French Gothic. *Photo: Oriel.*

83

*Above :* Three plate cupboards, late fifteenth century; that on the left is drawn from an illuminated MS. in the library of the Dukes of Burgundy, Brussels; the other examples from the King's Library, Paris. Compare the Gothic detail of the canopies with the architectural prototype below. Reproduced from Shaw's *Specimens of Ancient Furniture.*

*Right :* Pinnacles and tracery, west front, Rouen Cathedral, early sixteenth century. *Photo : Oriel.*

Oak standing cupboard for food, *circa* 1500. Three of the panels in front are pierced with tracery which corresponds to the last, the Perpendicular, period of English Gothic architecture. *Reproduced by courtesy of the Victoria and Albert Museum. Crown copyright.*

4*s*.' Coffers and chests were forerunners of safes, and were fitted with strong and often elaborate locks. Both the dug-out chests shown on page 80 have three locks, and the example from Kingstone, Herefordshire, is powerfully reinforced with iron bands. Chests with flat, hinged lids, like the boarded type on pages 11 and 81, were commodious storage places for clothes and linen, and as wealth and general security increased the amenities of life multiplied, especially in the prosperous walled trading towns of Europe, and the chest ceased to be a safe. Household treasures were no longer hidden and locked up; they could be openly displayed when not in use, and for this purpose the plate cupboard—literally a board for cups—was invented, with a superstructure called a desk on which silver vessels, cups and plates could stand. This evolved from stepped shelves, similar to those shown beyond the dais at the right of the coloured plate facing page 123, and became a piece of free-standing furniture with a cupboard below, and a pot board at or just above ground level, like the three French examples on the opposite page. The habit of displaying plate persisted, and in the late sixteenth and throughout the seventeenth centuries it was arranged on the open shelves of court cupboards, and later on dressers and sideboards. The court cupboard, dresser, and side-

85

Mid-fifteenth century oak chair, formerly the right-hand seat of a triple throne on the dais of the Great Hall, St Mary's Guildhall, Coventry. The throne, made for the Masters of the united guilds of St Mary, St John the Baptist, and St Catherine, has carved tracery that again corresponds to Perpendicular, English Gothic architecture. The carved finials represent the royal lions of England, and the arms of Coventry. Reproduced from Shaw's *Specimens of Ancient Furniture*.

board were descendants of the plate cupboard, though the mediaeval sideboard was a serving table, wholly different from the specialized type of side table with drawers and cupboards that was invented in the latter part of the eighteenth century.

By the close of the mediaeval period the design of seat furniture had greatly improved, though basketwork chairs used by peasants were still far more comfortable than the state chairs of kings, archbishops and great noblemen. A few chairs had concave backs, not unlike early nineteenth century tub chairs, and two examples are illustrated at the bottom of page 88; but those made by joiners were usually legless boxes, with severely upright backs and sides. The form may have been derived from choir stalls, for when individual stalls were detached from their place in the series, they became armchairs, like the privileged seats in the Greek theatre. The high-backed French ecclesiastical walnut seat on page 90 and the chair on the opposite page could both be units in a series of seats dependent on a backing wall. The fixed pews in churches may have been the prototypes for low-backed settles, like the example shown with a table dormante on page 76, while the high-backed settle had originally fitted into an alcove or a corner before becoming a free-standing seat of the type shown at the top of page 88. The angle

86

Fifteenth century church stalls at Holme Lacy, Herefordshire, with the hinged seats turned up, showing the misericord, the projecting bracket on the underside, that supported the occupant when leaning against it without actually allowing him to be seated. Choir stalls were usually constructed in series, as architectural conceptions, structurally related to and dependent on a wall; when a stall was separated from the series, and became a free-standing chair, it retained some of the characteristics of the stall, like the example shown below. (See also seats in the Greek theatre, page **20**.) *Reproduced from H.M. Inventory of the Royal Commission on Historical Monuments, Hereford-shire. By permission of the Controller, H.M. Stationery Office. Crown copyright.*

*Left:* Chair with panelled sides and moulded base and top rail. Fifteenth century. MS. Douce 371. fol. 127r. Bodleian.

A high-backed settle from a fifteenth century manuscript in the Bodleian Library. The finials and capping resemble those on the angle settle shown below. A small money chest or coffer stands on the table. MS. Bodley 283, fol. 59R.

*Left:* A fifteenth century interior, showing a chair with a concave back with turned spindles between the seat and top rail, and a bench in the background. MS. Douce 195, fol. 67V. Bodleian.

*Right:* A low-backed angle settle and a chair with a concave back. This could be the mediaeval forerunner of the Victorian cosy corner. (See page 178.) Drawn by F. W. Fairholt from the illuminated manuscript, *Boccace des Nobles Femmes.* Reproduced from *A History of Domestic Manners and Sentiments in England,* by Thomas Wright (1862).

Oak bookcase, with glazed doors. English, *circa* 1675. From Dyrham Park, Gloucestershire. This resembles the bookcase in the Pepys Library at Magdalene College, Cambridge. *Reproduced by courtesy of the Victoria and Albert Museum. Crown copyright.*

increase of household possessions. The press cupboard, used in halls and living rooms, was designed for storage, not display; the shelves on which vessels and dishes stood were concealed by panelled doors below and on the recessed superstructure; and the example on page 111 has secret receptacles in the pilasters that flank the central arcaded panel. Chests with two or three drawers in the base, like those on page 109, were the joiner's contribution to the development of the chest of drawers. All these improved cupboards and combinations of chests and cupboards were free-standing, and could be moved to new positions, so furnished rooms lost the air of stately and ponderous fixity that characterized the mediaeval interior.

Book presses that had formerly projected at right angles from the walls of libraries were replaced by open shelves extending from floor to ceiling, while independent cases with glazed doors housed smaller collections of books, like the example above. Until the Renaissance, the only educated people in many countries were churchmen and merchants; but when the ruling classes became literate, the widening of their civilized interests led to the expansion of libraries, and to improvements in the design of writing desks and cabinets. By the end of the seventeenth century the scrutoire or scriptoire, a

Late seventeenth century cabinet veneered with ivory, probably of Indo-Portuguese origin. At Ham House, Petersham, Surrey. Listed in the inventory. *Reproduced by courtesy of the Victoria and Albert Museum.*

114

*Above:* Late seventeenth century English scrutoire or scriptoire, veneered in walnut, shown open and closed. *In the possession of Mrs John Atkinson.*

*Left:* Late seventeenth century English cupboard in walnut, with fielded panels on the doors. The design and decoration suggest Portuguese influence.

*Above:* Oval table, the two leaves supported by double gates, with ringed baluster legs and stretchers. English, *circa* 1670. From Queen's College, Cambridge.

*Right:* Single leaf table with double gates with ball and reel turning on the legs. The leaf, which doubles the size of the top, folds back instead of dropping. English, country-made, late seventeenth century.

116

*Left :* Oak double leaf gate-leg table with 'barley-sugar' twist legs. *Circa* 1680. The ladder-back rush-bottomed chair in ash is mid-eighteenth century. *In the possession of Fleetwood Pritchard Esq.*

*Right :* Double gate-leg table in oak, *circa* 1670-90. The legs are slender versions of Tuscan columns. The classic orders were by this date far better understood by English furniture makers.

writing cabinet with a fall-down front, had appeared, also the bureau, with a hinged writing space or flap resting at an angle of 45° when closed. (An English scrutoire, veneered in walnut, is shown on page 115.)

Early in the sixteenth century the bedstead was separated from the wall, with the tester supported by a tall carved headboard and a pair of posts. The bedsteads on pages 104 and 105 are shown without the curtains which normally hung from rods concealed behind the frieze of the tester, ready to create an air-tight chamber when drawn. Half-tester bedsteads, with canopies bracketed forward from the headboard, known as early as the fifteenth century, were reintroduced late in the seventeenth; and another type, called a half-headed bedstead, had a headboard but no tester. The completely upholstered state beds on pages 106 and 107 are massive elaborations of the mediaeval type, with the framework completely hidden by luxurious fabrics. The truckle or trundle bed, low enough to be wheeled beneath a bedstead of ordinary size, was in use from the Middle Ages until the early nineteenth century, for children who slept in the same room as their parents, or for servants who had to be on duty at night.

Although long, heavy tables with six or eight legs connected by square-sectioned stretchers were made throughout the sixteenth and seventeenth centuries, their use was confined to a few large dining halls, mostly those of colleges and city companies: in contemporary inventories they are described as long tables, for the picturesque term refectory table is modern. Such pieces were too massive for the intimately furnished dining parlours, which unlike the great mediaeval halls were designed for privacy. Smaller extending tables were used, like the draw table on page 102, and the change from mediaeval seating arrangements, mentioned in chapter one, allowed dinner parties to be more relaxed and convivial, with the host and hostess at either end of the table

Oak chair-table, or 'table-chairwise'. The hinged back swings over to form a table. English, *circa* 1650-60. *Reproduced by courtesy of the Victoria and Albert Museum. Crown copyright.*

and the guests along the sides. Until the back-stool was invented in the late sixteenth century, guests sat on benches or joint stools, the host (and sometimes the hostess) alone having the privilege of a chair. The draw-table was a space-saving device, so was the drop-leaf table with single or double hinged leaves supported by folding arms or hinged gate-legs, like those on pages 116 and 117. The chair-table, mentioned in the previous chapter, was also a space saver, and a rectangular mid-seventeenth century type is shown above.

A back-stool, as the name implies, was simply a stool fitted with a back: when first introduced it was not thought of as a chair because it was armless; later it was called a single or side chair to distinguish it from a chair with arms, which was then called an arming chair or an armchair. Back-stool survived as a chair-maker's term until the second half of the eighteenth century. The basic type, common alike to England, France and Holland, is shown on page 119 opposite, and the assumption that the broad-seated back-stool was first made to accommodate the farthingale is probably sound. That vast hooped dress was fashionable in the late sixteenth and early seventeenth centuries, but the name farthingale chair is another picturesque modern invention. The English chair from Denham place, on page 121, with the turned walnut frame and

118

Two joined armchairs, English, early seventeenth century.

*Above, left :* From Brimfield Church, Herefordshire. Compare with the example on page 16.

*Above, right :* From Ledbury Church, Herefordshire. The carving on the back panels has a brisk vitality, but the carver has not mastered Renaissance ornament, and the vine leaves and tendrils on the seat rail are early Tudor in character. *Both examples reproduced from H.M. Inventories of the Royal Commission on Historical Monuments, Herefordshire. By permission of the Controller of H.M. Stationery Office. Crown copyright.*

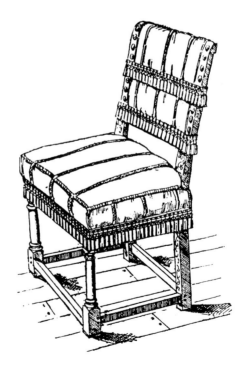

*Right :* An early seventeenth century upholstered back-stool, the so-called 'farthingale' chair. The turned front legs follow the proportions of a Roman Doric column. Drawn from an example at Knole Park by Charles Lock Eastlake and reproduced from his *Hints on Household Taste* (second edition, 1869), page 77.

119

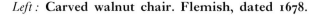

*Left :* **Carved walnut chair. Flemish, dated 1678.**

*Below, centre :* **Carved and turned ebony chair, Indo-Dutch, from Batavia.** *Circa* **1660.** *Both examples reproduced by courtesy of the Victoria and Albert Museum. Crown copyright.*

*Below, right :* **Dutch roundabout or burgomaster chair, a type made in the East Indies for sale in Europe in the late seventeenth and early eighteenth centuries. From Henry Shaw's** *Specimens of Ancient Furniture.*

embroidered seat and back, was made about 1660 and shows how the basic shape of the early back-stools remained unchanged.

The heavy joined armchairs, like those on page 16 and the top of page 119, were replaced by lighter and more graceful shapes with carved and turned frames, and arms curved in length, depth and breadth. Such refinements followed the establishment of chair-making as a separate craft. As the joiner's influence waned, mediaeval rigidity disappeared. In France the suite had been invented, consisting of matching chairs, stools and couches, sometimes numbering as many as twenty-four chairs and stools and two or four couches. Suites of upholstered chairs had existed in the reign of Elizabeth I, and after the mid-seventeenth century the suite was designed in relation to interior decoration, which brought furnishing into a closer relationship with architecture. As upholstery improved, comfort increased, and such agreeable invitations to indolence as the sleeping chair began to undermine dignity of posture.

The unsuspected conflict between dignity and comfort continued, and in the third quarter of the seventeenth century the high-backed, winged arm chair appeared, so obviously designed for relaxation that it was called an easy chair. The wings which flanked the back were also known as lugs or cheeks; they gave protection from draughts, and the arms were either open with padded elbows or continuous with the seat and scrolled outwards, like the example on page 53. This was the ancestor of all the easy chairs that have since changed our attitudes and established our standards of comfort.

*Above, left :* Late seventeenth century carved and turned arm chair, from Michael-church, Escley, Herefordshire. *Reproduced from H.M. Inventories of the Royal Commission on Historical Monuments, Herefordshire. By permission of the Controller of H.M. Stationery Office. Crown copyright.*

*Above, right :* Carved and turned walnut arm chair, with caned seat and back panels. *Circa* **1670.** *Reproduced by courtesy of the Victoria and Albert Museum. Crown copyright.*

*Left :* Turned and joined walnut chair, *circa* **1650.**

*Centre :* Late seventeenth century chair from Farringdon Within, London.

*Right :* Turned walnut and embroidered chair, *circa* **1660,** from Denham Place, Buckinghamshire. The embroidery dates from about **1641-55.** *Examples at left and right are reproduced by courtesy of the Victoria and Albert Museum : centre subject from H.M. Inventories of the Royal Commission on Historical Monuments, London, Vol IV. By permission of the Controller of H.M. Stationery Office. Crown copyright.*

Pair of 'Sleeping Chayres' with carved and gilded frames, upholstered in cherry-coloured brocade. The backs, fitted with iron ratchets, may be adjusted for reclining. At Ham House, Petersham, Surrey. *Reproduced by courtesy of the Victoria and Albert Museum. Crown copyright.*

The day-bed, known in the early sixteenth century, was a long seat with one or two ends, either fixed or adjustable. Day-beds resembled couches, though the couch usually had a back and one or two ends. (Couche was the mediaeval term for bed.) Another long seat was the settee intended for two or more people, with the back often formed by two conjoined chair backs. Settees were introduced during the second half of the seventeenth century, and an upholstered type came into use later, resembling the low-backed settle in form, though far less austere as a seat. The two types of settle, mentioned in the previous chapter, had developed, without benefit of upholstery, into something far more comfortable and decorative than their mediaeval forerunners. Although the basic form persisted, the advance in the joiner's skill and sense of proportion may be judged by comparing the settles on the page opposite, which date from the late seventeenth or early eighteenth century, with those illustrated on pages 76 and 88, which belong to the Gothic tradition.

The age of elegance in furniture design was generated in the mid-seventeenth century, when the arts of the Far East began to exert a refining influence on form and colour, and European craftsmen, particularly in Holland, reinforced their own inventiveness with stimulating ideas drawn from China, Japan and India.

Royal Egyptian furniture of the fourteenth century B.C., from the tomb of Tutankhamen, preserved in the Cairo Museum.

*Above:* Miniature painted chest with domed lid. Height: $17\frac{3}{8}$ in; length: 24 in; breadth: 17 in. The chest is of wood, coated with a form of gesso, on which spirited scenes of war and hunting are painted. The side illustrated shows Tutankhamen in his war chariot.

*Right:* A cabinet of cedar-wood and ebony, gilded and decorated with hieroglyphic symbols. Bronze hinges are used for the top. The general form anticipates the small chests with stands produced by French and English cabinet-makers during the eighteenth century, but without the grace of the latter. Egyptian furniture relied more on richness of decoration than elegance of line.

Both subjects are included in *Tutankhamen*, by Christiane Desroches-Noblecourt, published by The Connoisseur and Michael Joseph, 1963, and are reproduced by courtesy of F. L. Kenett for George Rainbird Limited.

Interior of a fifteenth century hall. At the right a high-backed seat of state, with a curved canopy suspended above, stands on the dais, and beyond a buffet or plate cup-board projects at right angles from the wall, with a small platform behind for the butler. At the left, some guests are seated on a form with a rich fabric hanging on the wall behind them, others on a low-backed settle. Luxury in mediaeval furnishing depended on the lavish use of brilliant fabrics, not on the elaborate decoration of furniture. *Reproduced from a MS. of Quintus Curtius in the Bodleian Library* (751 f 127R).

Settle of chestnut wood, with high, concave back and cupboards below the seat. Late seventeenth or early eighteenth century. *Copyright 'Country Life'*.

Oak settle, with top rail and front stretchers carved with foliage. Late seventeenth or early eighteenth century. *In the possession of John Atkinson, Esq., F.R.I.B.A.*

Three of a set of seven chairs with cane seats and japanned frames, decorated with Chinese motifs. In the Blue Drawing Room at Ham House, Petersham, Surrey.

CHAPTER SIX

# The Magnificent Century

**B**EFORE the second half of the seventeenth century, nearly all seats, tables, and receptacles were rectilinear, bounded by straight lines, often abruptly angular in appearance, though occasionally softened and relieved by carved ornament, which disguised but did not change a fundamental severity of outline. Coffer-makers' chairs with their flowing X-shaped frames, and the floridly carved baroque tables and cabinet stands were the exceptions; but a structural inheritance from mediaeval models remained, until early in the eighteenth century rigidity was dispelled by a new, curvilinear conception of design which revolutionized the form of furniture as the introduction of veneering had revolutionized its character. The cabriole leg, which gracefully united opposing curves—convex above, concave below—was introduced, and in the hands of Dutch, French and English craftsmen became part of a curvilinear composition, instead of an isolated support, based on a stylized natural form like the Greek and Roman examples on pages 20 and 68. The subtle relationship of curves in this new form of design is shown on the next page by the front and side views of a bended-back single chair, while the two chairs on page 127, and the settee on page 129, show how the development of curvilinear design released seat furniture from structural dependence on underframing, after makers had discovered that weight could be distributed just as efficiently and far more elegantly by curved as by straight legs. This principle of distributing weight had long been latent in the X-shaped frame; but the adoption of the cabriole leg, while changing established ideas about stability, could not alone have generated such a revolution in design.

Commerce with the Far East had stimulated the imagination of European craftsmen, and R. W. Symonds has described the Chinese original of the bended-back chair, which had a splat bent to accommodate the curve of the human back and a top rail shaped

The transition from rectilinear to curvilinear design is shown by the contrast between the stiff, upright, high-backed chairs of the late seventeenth century and the bended-back chairs of the early eighteenth.

*Left :* **One of a pair of carved walnut single chairs, English,** *circa* **1690.** *Reproduced by courtesy of the Victoria and Albert Museum. Crown copyright.*

*Right :* **This bended-back single chair is an early example of curvilinear design. Walnut, with cabriole front legs, splayed back legs, turned stretchers, a back gracefully curved to invite a relaxed posture, and a drop-in rush seat. This is typical of the chairs made in England during the opening decades of the eighteenth century.** *In the possession of the author.*

126

The development of curvilinear design is shown by these two English armchairs, separated in time by about twenty years.

*Left :* **Walnut armchair with upholstered seat and back, scroll-over arms and cabriole legs,** *circa* **1710.** *Reproduced by permission of the Syndics of the Fitzwilliam Museum, Cambridge.*

*Right :* **Carved mahogany armchair, with a wide seat,** *circa* **1730. The cushion (which is not original) covers a canework seat.** *Reproduced by courtesy of the Trustees of Sir John Soane's Museum.*

like a milk-maid's yoke. Chairs of this type were imported into England by the East India Company; and the relaxed posture they invited was as acceptable to the English nobility and gentry as to the Dutch bourgeoisie. The severe lines dictated by the needs of dignity disappeared when those who sponsored fashions in England tacitly admitted that dignity and comfort could both be served by seat furniture; an admission never made by the French aristocracy, whose manners continued to be exquisitely artificial though their habits remained frankly, even crudely natural, as Saint-Simon's memoirs of the court of Louis XIV reveal, though the character of French furniture reveals even more. Not that curvilinear design was rejected by French chair-makers and *ébénistes*; the fashion for curving the fronts and sides of cabinets and commodes originated in France, and this *bombé* furniture with its swelling convexities was elegant, when French, comfortable and commodious, when Dutch, and never exaggerated, when English. Makers had everywhere mastered the classic idiom; their work was related

The revolutionary changes in the technique of English furniture design between the reigns of Charles II and George I are illustrated by these two walnut day-beds.

*Above:* The florid carving on the back, frame and side stretchers adorns a rigid and severe shape. *Circa* 1685.

*Below:* The adjustable back has two vase-shaped splats separated by a turned baluster, the uprights end in volutes, and the four cabriole legs are lightly carved on the knees. New graces have been achieved without reliance on the carver's art. For instance, there is no abrupt break between the angle of the back and the legs, as in the upper example; the back uprights and the splayed back legs form a continuous line. *Circa* 1715.

*Both subjects reproduced by courtesy of the Victoria and Albert Museum. Crown copyright.*

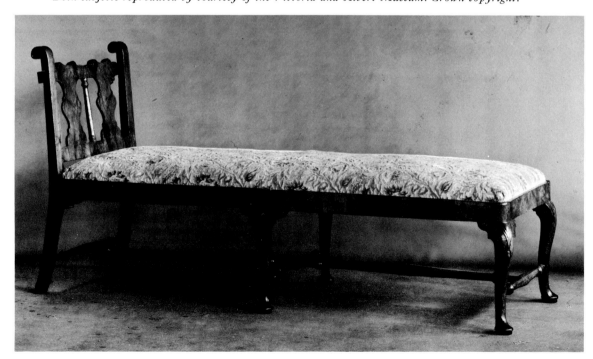

English settee of carved walnut, with upholstered seat and back. First quarter of the eighteenth century. The arm supports spring boldly outwards from the seat rail in sharp contrast with the gentle curves of the cabriole legs. The designer has achieved contrast without conflict. The arms scroll over to terminate in the heads of eagles; the acanthus scrolls on the knees of the legs and the shells that rise into the seat rail are lightly carved, and the claw-and-ball feet are bold and vigorous. A delicately moulded frame encloses the upholstered back. *Reproduced by courtesy of the Victoria and Albert Museum. Crown copyright.*

to current architectural design and interior decoration; their skill allowed them to accommodate within the classic framework the waves of taste that frothed and bubbled over Europe without injuring the good proportions or structural probity of the things they made.

These discoveries in design were accompanied and accentuated by the rococo style of decoration, invented in France, and originating, as strap-work had originated over a century and a half earlier, in two dimensions. The initial inspiration of the style has been attributed to Pierre Le Pautre, a designer and engraver, whose father, Jean Le Pautre, had followed the same craft and worked in the baroque style. Rococo was derived from the French word *rocaille*, or 'rock-work', which was used to describe the artificial grottos and fountains in the gardens of Versailles; but the term did not become current until the nineteenth century, when it denoted excessively ornate furniture and carved decoration, and was identified with the style of Louis XV. For a long time rococo remained a linear art, but the craftsmen who gave it three-dimensional life, the carvers and *ciseleurs*, worked for patrons whose taste for splendour encouraged ornamental excesses. Rococo acquired a febrile gaiety that accurately reflected the importance of trivialities in the graceful (but far from comfortable) life of the French Court and the aristocracy. Designers working in the style borrowed and incorporated Chinese decorative motifs, for there was a subtle affinity between rococo and ancient Chinese culture. Although classic motifs were used, and classic proportions honoured, the style was essentially asymmetrical, though on furniture this characteristic quality was often confined to the chased and gilt mounts of bronze, like those applied to the centre of the chest of drawers on page 131.

As rococo developed, curvilinear design was over-emphasized. What began as a style of decoration, ended by appropriating the form and visually denying the purpose

One of a pair of marriage coffers, with an arched top and concave sides, veneered on oak with ebony and Boulle marquetry of engraved brass on tortoise-shell, with bronze mounts, chased and gilt. Each table on which the coffer stands, has a drawer in front. The decorative treatment shows how completely the classical idiom had been mastered by the French *ébéniste* of the late seventeenth and early eighteenth centuries. These coffers were probably made for a member of the French royal family, though the crown, vases and feet may have been added later. *Reproduced by courtesy of the Trustees of the Wallace Collection. Crown copyright.*

In an age of classical regularity and symmetrical features, the revolutionary rococo style introduced asymmetrical ornamental forms, as exemplified by the bronze mounts, chased and gilt, on this chest of drawers of oak, veneered with kingwood and mahogany, made in 1739 for the bed-chamber of Louis XV at Versailles. *Reproduced by courtesy of the Trustees of the Wallace Collection. Crown copyright.*

of furniture. A style dedicated to luxury tended to minimize utility and magnify decorative character; and in France throughout the fifty-nine years of Louis XV's reign the design of furniture illustrated the progressive rejection of realities by a gay, irresponsible society. Superb workmanship was lavished on the chairs, tables, secretaires, cabinets and screens that furnished galleries, saloons and boudoirs. In bedrooms by far the most important article was the toilet table, where hours were spent by ladies before they could confidently exhibit their charms in the stifling, candle-lit rooms of royal palaces and great mansions. With hairdressers, maids, and often a Negro page in attendance, these prolonged preparations for displaying youthful beauty or disguising age, were conducted with urbane publicity, for friends of both sexes were admitted to the spectacle, so the main business of the day, the exchange of gossip and court scandal, could begin early. (Hogarth has recorded an English version of such an informal reception in his painting, reproduced on page 134, of 'The Countess's Dressing-Room', in the 'Marriage à la Mode' series.) Those elegant ladies and gentlemen never washed; they believed that water injured the skin; the minute size of bason stands even at the end of the eighteenth century, and the increasing complexity of toilet tables show a prolonged loyalty to paint and powder; soap was used by valets and barbers when shaving their masters, but was seldom used for anything else. Cotton wool, dipped in spirits of wine and patted lightly over the body, took the place of ablutions. A Roman patrician, while recognizing and possibly approving of the classical setting of high life in the eighteenth

Looking glass with a carved and gilded wood frame. English, *circa* 1730. The affinity with architectural design is obvious; classical motifs are used with vigorous confidence, and the proportions are impeccable. Compare this with the rococo example on the opposite page. *Reproduced by courtesy of the Victoria and Albert Museum. Crown copyright.*

Two examples of English rococo.

*Left*: A carved and gilt mirror, of mid-eighteenth century design, inspired by if not actually the work of Thomas Chippendale. *In the collection of the late Sir Albert Richardson, PP. R.A., at Avenue House, Ampthill.*

*Right*: A girandole, from *The Gentleman and Cabinet-Maker's Director*, by Thomas Chippendale (1754).

The English commode in the French taste on page 38 is another example of the Anglicized rococo style.

Mid-eighteenth century Chinese throne of carved red lacquer, made for the Emperor Ch'ien Lung (1736-1795). The colour is warm red, with a background, visible behind the intricately carved decoration, of dark sage green. The folding black lacquer screen at the back is also Chinese, *circa* **1722**. *Reproduced by courtesy of the Victoria and Albert Museum.*

An early Georgian interior, painted by William Hogarth, showing the Assembly at Wanstead House. The decoration and furniture are attributed to William Kent (? 1685-1748); the house was designed by Colin Campbell in 1715; and the painting, commissioned in 1727, was probably finished in the fourth decade of the eighteenth century. *From the McFadden Collection in the Philadelphia Museum of Art.*

Hogarth's painting of the interior at Wanstead House, reproduced on the coloured plate opposite, includes ornately carved and gilt furniture, attributed, like the decoration of the room, to William Kent. Such florid carving was characteristic of the early Georgian period in England, and the examples of Kent's work on this page are reproduced from plates 43 (*above*) and 41 (*below*) of *Some Designs of Mr Inigo Jones and Mr Wm Kent*, published in 1744 by John Vardy.

*Left :* **Candle-stand in mahogany with scrolled feet. Early eighteenth century.** *In the possession of R. G. Carruthers Esq. Copyright 'Oriel'.*

*Centre :* **Candle-stand from** *The Gentleman and Cabinet-Maker's Director,* **by Thomas Chippendale (1754). Compare with the late seventeenth century candle stands from Knole Park on page 59.**

*Right :* **Gueridon Table, veneered on the sides with floral designs, and containing a cupboard. French, Louis XVI period.** *Reproduced by courtesy of the Trustees of the Wallace Collection. Crown copyright.*

to town fashions, is the Windsor chair, which by anticipating the technique of mass-production is the only article that has survived the industrial revolution unmarred. This type of chair, with turned spindles socketed into a shaped seat, probably originated during the second half of the seventeenth century, in some locality, such as Buckinghamshire, where many acres of beech woods could provide the material. Windsor has become a generic name for this type of stick furniture, and was first used in 1724, according to *The Dictionary of English Furniture.* The illustrations on pages 164, 165 and 61 show the progress of the type from primitive forerunners to the graceful double bow-backs with cabriole legs. Evolved and perfected in rustic workshops, the Windsor may be regarded as the national chair of England as the rocker is the national chair of America.

The Windsor chair was a triumph of common sense and comfort; and although an almost excessive slenderness characterized much of the seat furniture made towards the end of the century, comfort was given more attention, though never at the expense of good proportions. Apart from seat furniture, many articles were perfected which

The dining-room at Belgrave Hall, Leicester. The Hall was built between 1709 and 1713, and this panelled room dates from the second decade of the eighteenth century, though it has since been repaired in places. The room is furnished with mid and late eighteenth century examples. The chairs are typical of those made by Thomas Chippendale and his contemporaries; the serpentine-fronted mahogany sideboard and the knife boxes on it, are about 1770-90, and the dining table with the pillar and tripod supports, 1790-1800. At the right in the corner is a china cabinet with a pagoda top, a tribute to the 'Chinese Taste' of the mid-eighteenth century. *Reproduced by courtesy of the City of Leicester Museum and Art Gallery.*

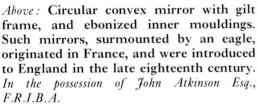

*Above:* **Circular convex mirror with gilt frame, and ebonized inner mouldings. Such mirrors, surmounted by an eagle, originated in France, and were introduced to England in the late eighteenth century.** *In the possession of John Atkinson Esq., F.R.I.B.A.*
*Right:* **Console table of carved and gilded pine, with marbled plinth and marble top. English,** *circa* **1730.** *Reproduced by courtesy of the Victoria and Albert Museum. Crown copyright.*

increased not only comfort and convenience but tidiness. The sideboard had become a graceful side table, like the example opposite from Hepplewhite's *Guide*; and a more commodious type was introduced, with drawers for cutlery and silver, cupboards for glass, and sometimes a small, inconspicuous cupboard at the side for a chamber pot. A serpentine-fronted sideboard with a central drawer flanked by cupboards is shown on page 157, in the dining room at Belgrave Hall. Those miniature cases for wine called cellarets often stood below the sideboard. (An octagonal example is included in George Morland's painting reproduced on page 149.) In kitchens and occasionally in dining rooms a haster was used; a tall, metal-lined cupboard of deal with an open back, which could be placed against a fire, the doors shut, and plates on the racks and shelves kept warm. The extending dining table was invented; different in mechanism and design from the earlier draw-table, for leaves could be inserted to give additional length; there were also specialized types, such as the breakfast table and the kidney-shaped social table, with a revolving, cylindrical receptacle for wine bottles, so three or four people could enjoy their wine by the fireside. (Examples of both are shown on page 153.)

The chest and the tallboy, or double chest, contributed at least theoretically to the

*Above :* One of a pair of side tables designed by Robert Adam, 1765, formerly in the piers of the Long Gallery at Croome Court, Worcestershire, and now in the Philadelphia Museum of Art. *National Buildings Record copyright.*

*Left :* Sideboard from *The Cabinet-Maker and Upholsterer's Guide*, by A. Hepplewhite and Co. (London: 1788).

159

Makers in remote country districts, seldom influenced by current fashions, continued to use and improve old forms. The traditional furniture of Wales, for example, changed little between the mid seventeenth century and the early nineteenth. (See page 44.)

*Above, left :* A regional development of the press cupboard, with three tiers instead of two, this tridarn, from Llanberis, Caernarvonshire, has the date 1695 carved on the arcaded panel. (See page 111.)

*Above, right :* A combined bacon cupboard and settle in elm with four drawers below the seat and fielded panels on the doors. Mid-eighteenth century: made in West Wales.

*Below, right :* Chest with drawers below on stand with turned legs and curved stretchers. Made of pine inlaid with sycamore, and dated 1734. From Milford Haven, Pembrokeshire.

*All three examples reproduced by permission of the National Museum of Wales, Welsh Folk Museum.*

*Above :* **Early Georgian chest, carved and gilt gesso, from Shobdon Court, Hereford-shire.** *Circa* **1720. Compare the florid carving with the furniture by William Kent on page 155.** *Reproduced by courtesy of the Victoria and Albert Museum. Crown copyright.*
*Below :* **Mahogany blanket chest, with drawers in the base and bracket feet. English, circa 1750.** *Reproduced by permission of the Syndics of the Fitzwilliam Museum, Cambridge.*

161

*Above, left:* Serpentine-fronted mahogany chest of drawers. *Circa* **1760.** *Reproduced by courtesy of the Victoria and Albert Museum. Crown copyright.*
*Above, right:* Serpentine-fronted mahogany chest, with fluted angles. *Circa* **1740–50.** The top drawer is fitted for use as a dressing or writing table. *Formerly in the collection of the late Robert Atkinson, F.R.I.B.A.*

162

*Left:* A mahogany tallboy, with vertical fluting on the angles of the upper part. *Circa* **1740–50.** The mirror has a mahogany frame, surmounted by a swan-neck broken pediment; mouldings and carving are gilded. *Circa* **1730.** The chair, of Chippendale type, is carved in low relief. *Circa* **1760–70.** *Formerly in the collection of the late Robert Atkinson, F.R.I.B.A.*
*Right:* Walnut tallboy, *circa* **1725–30.** Compare with the earlier example on page 28. *In the possession of John Atkinson, Esq., F.R.I.B.A.*

*Left :* China cabinet of carved mahogany in the 'Gothic taste', *circa* **1760-70.** *Reproduced by courtesy of the Victoria and Albert Museum. Crown copyright.*
*Right :* Cedar-lined press in mahogany, *circa* **1740.** The swan-neck pediment, fluted pilasters, and cornice show the controlling influence of classic architecture on design. *Formerly in the collection of the late Robert Atkinson, F.R.I.B.A.*

163

*Left :* French commode, with serpentine front and sides, veneered on deal with ebony and Boulle marquetry of brass on tortoiseshell. The bronze mounts are chased and gilt. Late eighteenth century.
*Right :* French bow-fronted corner cupboard of oak, stained black and veneered with a panel of Chinese lacquer, framed in acanthus scrolls. Rococo exuberance is well under control. Second half of the eighteenth century. *Both examples reproduced by courtesy of the Trustees of the Wallace Collection.*

Primitive forerunners of the stick-back chair, from which the Windsor type developed.
*Right :* Three-legged chair from Melinbyrhedyn, Montgomeryshire.
*Far right :* Chair from Llangeitho, Cardiganshire. First half of eighteenth century.
*Both subjects reproduced by permission of the National Museum of Wales, Welsh Folk Museum.*

Types of stick-back Windsor chairs: mid-eighteenth to mid-nineteenth century. *From left to right :* **Double bow-back; comb-back, with cabriole legs; wheel-back; baluster splat; and smoker's bow.**

tidiness of bedrooms and dressing rooms; and cabinet-makers were ingenious in devising an almost bewildering variety of desks and writing tables, for letter-writing was a form of artistic expression at which Georgian ladies and gentlemen excelled, and no room was fully furnished unless there were facilities for writing. Toilet and dressing tables could also be used for writing, like those on pages 141 and 142; shallow screen writing desks, with a fall front above and a cupboard below, could stand close to a fireplace, so the feet remained warm and the complexion inviolate; and innumerable small, compact desks and cabinets were made for ladies, such as the sheveret or cheveret. (Both screen writing desks and sheverets are illustrated on page 152.) In libraries large bookcases were often made with a central escritoire drawer, like the mid-Georgian type on page 144; and there were many variations of escritoire and bureau bookcases, of which a few are shown on page 145. By the end of the century the cylinder fall desk was in use (one is shown open and closed on page 147), and the tambour had been invented; this consisted of thin strips of moulded wood with the flat side glued to linen or canvas forming a flexible shutter with a reeded surface which ran in guiding grooves, and was used for desk tops and occasionally for cupboard doors.

In architecture and furniture design, the eighteenth century in Europe may be justly described as the magnificent century. The character of magnificence varied with

*Above, left :* **One of a set of six low-backed Windsor chairs in mahogany,** *circa* **1760-70. At Ham House, Petersham, Surrey.** *Reproduced by courtesy of the Victoria and Albert Museum. Centre :* **Oak writing chair,** *circa* **1720.** *In the possession of Julian Gloag, Esq. Right :* **Early eighteenth century shaving chair. This is the same design as the writing chair with a head-rest rising from the yoke rail.**

Two bow-backed Windsor chairs, with spur stretchers. The example with cabriole legs is late eighteenth century; the smaller chair, early nineteenth. *Both in the possession of John Atkinson, Esq., F.R.I.B.A.*

the country: in France, as society steadily advanced towards dissolution, it became frantic; in the etiquette-ridden states of Germany, oppressive; in Austria and Italy, gay; in England, restrained, but consistently gracious.

165

*Left and centre :* Single chairs of carved mahogany, with cabriole legs and claw-and-ball feet, of the type made by Thomas Chippendale and his contemporaries. The bended-back chair (*right*) of the Queen Anne period had bequeathed its grace of form to makers in the middle years of the eighteenth century (See pages 126 and 127.) *Reproduced by courtesy of R. G. Carruthers, Esq.*

The cabriole leg was replaced by a leg of square section after the mid-eighteenth century, with stretchers at the sides and back.
*Left :* Chair with dipped seat, *circa* **1760**. *Reproduced by courtesy of R. G. Carruthers, Esq.*
*Centre :* Although the outline of the chair-back is similar in the Chippendale types shown on this page, the pierced splat was greatly and ingeniously varied.
*Right :* Country-made elbow chair, with flat, pierced splat. *Circa* **1760**. *Reproduced by courtesy of Mrs W. Bulmer. Photographs copyright 'Oriel'.*

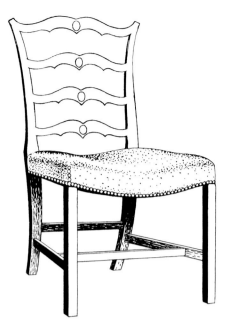

*Left :* Country-made simplified version of a Chippendale single chair.
*Centre :* The town maker's elaboration of the (*right*) country-made ladder-back, rush-bottomed chair. Compare with the fourteenth century prototype on page 92. *Chairs at left and right are in the collection of Bruce Allsopp, Esq., F.R.I.B.A.*

*Left :* Bow-backed armchair with wheatsheaf splat, *circa* **1770-75**. *Reproduced by courtesy of Mrs W. Bulmer.*
*Centre :* Oval-backed armchair with pierced splat and bars forming the outline of the anthemion ornament. *Circa* **1780-85**.
*Right :* Shield-back armchair, with painted decoration. *Circa* **1780-85**. *Reproduced by courtesy of R. G. Carruthers, Esq. Photographs copyright 'Oriel'.*

*Left:* Armchair of pinewood, carved and gilt, upholstered with embroidered silk, French: Louis XVI.
*Centre:* Armchair of carved birch, gilt, and upholstered with Beauvais tapestry. French: Louis XVI. *Both subjects reproduced by courtesy of the Trustees of the Wallace Collection. Crown copyright.*
*Right:* English armchair, contemporary with the French examples. *Reproduced by courtesy of R. G. Carruthers, Esq. Copyright 'Oriel'.*

168     Two armchairs, *circa* 1790–95, of the type designed by Thomas Sheraton.
*Left:* Frame japanned black, decorated with gold.
*Right:* Satinwood frame, painted and decorated with floral motifs. *In the possession of Mrs V. Atkins.*

*Left :* **In** *The Universal System of Household Furniture* (**1759-63**), Ince and Mayhew included some asymmetrical designs for small settees, called French corner chairs, on which rococo ornament was used, but with great restraint.
*Right :* Imported oriental furniture continued to exert an exotic influence on European taste. This example, one of a set of four Anglo-Indian chairs of carved ivory, is late eighteenth century, and a refined version of the Dutch round-about or burgomaster chair, on page 120. The frame follows the European style, but much of the ornament is Indian. *Reproduced by courtesy of the Trustees of Sir John Soane's Museum.*

**A sofa designed by Robert Adam for Sir Laurence Dundas, 1764. Classical ornament delicately emphasizes the lines of the frame, and the anthemion device surmounts the cresting on the back, and appears on the knees of the cabriole legs and the curved arms.** *Reproduced from the original drawing in Sir John Soane's Museum by courtesy of the Trustees.*

169

The collector and the antiquary influenced fashionable taste in many European countries, but particularly in England. Horace Walpole filled his Gothic villa at Strawberry Hill with mediaeval fragments, and wealthy men like Charles Towneley (1737-1805) were attracted by classical art, travelling to Italy and Sicily to collect antique marbles. This painting by Johann Zoffany shows Towneley in his study, about 1792. *Reproduced by courtesy of the County Borough of Burnley Art Gallery and Museum.*

*Above:* Bookcase unit, with recess below. The walnut sideboard has fielded panels on the doors. The circular table is in brown oak. Designed by Sir Gordon Russell. (See page 6.)

*Left:* Ladder-back chair in yew, designed and made by Sir Gordon Russell. *In the possession of Mrs John Gloag.* A twentieth century interpretation of a traditional form. (See pages 92, 117, and 167.)

189

With this modular living-room furniture, an old partnership with the wall is resumed. Designed by Christopher Heal, F.S.I.A., this range of panels, bookcases and storage units, is veneered in teak, with solids in afrormosia, and the backs of the bookcases painted black. The use of such units frees floor space. *By courtesy of Heal and Son Ltd.*

making class at the Bauhaus at Dessau. An entirely new way of thought about design created an effective revolution, not a false one like that attempted by the exponents of Art Nouveau, for structural changes followed the use of industrially-produced materials, and as the characteristics of those materials and the nature of mechanical processes were common to all countries, the idea of an international style seemed plausible. The change from rectilinear to curvilinear design had been gradual, and was carried out when wood was the principal material; but the new structural changes were sudden and uncompromisingly revolutionary, for they ended the traditional dependence of furniture-makers on wood, and compelled designers to reassess functional needs. As usual, furniture design was following a contemporary architectural trend, and entering a period of functionalism, when M. Le Corbusier's dictum, 'A House is a Machine for living in', was all powerful, and its inhuman implications were as yet undetected. That rather bleak phase of functionalism in design, accompanied by a total rejection of ornament and an optimistic reliance on the intrinsic decorative qualities of materials, was followed by the development of what we now call the contemporary style, which has appeared, with marked national characteristics, in most European countries, England and the United States.

Furniture in the third quarter of the twentieth century is resuming its former partnership with the wall: free-standing articles, with their heavy framework and large claim on floor space, have been replaced by ranges of shelves and storage units, like the example opposite; the design of modern rooms facilitates the use of such compact, fitted furniture, and the disappearance of the fireplace has changed the arrangement and character of seating as they were changed over five hundred years ago when the open fire on a central hearth was abandoned in favour of the fireplace. Seats are moulded to human contours, like the example of curvilinear design in birch plywood by Alvar Aalto on page 60 and the armchair of plastic resin reinforced with Fiberglass by Charles Eames on page 61, while contemporary upholstery transcends anything imagined by the most comfort-loving Victorian. Comfort has finally vanquished dignity.

Although people have not changed their shape during the last two or three centuries, they are a little taller, their personal habits have altered greatly, generally for the better, they are probably less placid than their forefathers, and in furnishing are concerned more with temporary convenience than permanent possessions. Such preferences are satisfied by the sprightly elegance and efficiency of contemporary furniture. Skill has not been banished by machinery: it has been changed and turned into new channels.

No machine can give to furniture the peculiar excellence that craftsmen who thought with their hands could give to the things they made; but machines, intelligently directed, and industrially-produced materials, imaginatively used, can give us a different kind of excellence.

This survey has attempted to show how faithfully the design of furniture reflects the character of society in any age and in various countries; how skill has developed, and how often it has been stimulated or repressed by fashion; but the subject is vast, and this is no more than an outline.

*Left:* Upholstered easy chair, designed by the late Ernest Race, R.D.I., PP.S.I.A., which received a Design Centre award in 1959. Made by Race Furniture Limited. *Copyright: The Council of Industrial Design.*
*Right:* Club chair, designed for Hille by Robin Day, R.D.I., F.S.I.A. The buttoned seat and back cushions are on 4 inch Latex Foam. The seat cushion is supported on rubber webbing. The underframe is of stainless steel with Nylon-tipped legs.

# BOOKS FOR REFERENCE

*The Dictionary of English Furniture*, revised and enlarged by Ralph Edwards, c.b.e., f.s.a. Three volumes. London: Country Life Ltd, 1954.

*The Shorter Dictionary of English Furniture*, by Ralph Edwards, c.b.e., f.s.a. London: Country Life Ltd, 1964.

*A Short Dictionary of Furniture*, by John Gloag, f.s.a. London: George Allen & Unwin Ltd, 1952. Abridged, paper-back edition, 1966. New, revised American edition, Holt, Rinehart and Winston, Inc., New York, 1965.

*Dictionnaire de L'Ameublement et de La Décoration*, by H. Havard. Four volumes. Paris: Maison Quantin.

*The Practical Decoration of Furniture*, by H. P. Shapland, a.r.i.b.a. Three volumes. London: Ernest Benn Ltd, 1926.

*Furniture Making in Seventeenth and Eighteenth Century England*, by R. W. Symonds. London: The Connoisseur, 1955.

*Furniture*, by F. J. B. Watson, b.a., f.s.a. Wallace Collection Catalogues. London: Hertford House, 1956.

*The London Furniture Makers*, 1660–1840, by Sir Ambrose Heal. London: B. T. Batsford Ltd, 1953.

*The Country Life Book of English Furniture*, by Edward T. Joy. London: Country Life Ltd, 1964.

*English Furniture*, by John Gloag, f.s.a. London: A. & C. Black Ltd (The Library of English Art), fifth edition, revised and enlarged, 1965.

*Victorian Furniture*, by R. W. Symonds and B. B. Whineray. London: Country Life Ltd, 1962.

*Furniture from Machines*, by Gordon Logie, a.r.i.b.a. London: George Allen & Unwin Ltd, 1947.

*Pioneers of Modern Design*, by Nikolaus Pevsner, c.b.e., f.s.a. New York: The Museum of Modern Art, 1949. New edition, Penguin Books Ltd, 1960.